P9-CTQ-966

THE DETLING SECRET

Also by Julian Symons

THE DETLING SECRET

JULIAN SYMONS

THE VIKING PRESS
NEW YORK

Copyright © 1982 by Julian Symons
All rights reserved
Published in 1983 by The Viking Press
625 Madison Avenue, New York, N.Y. 10022
Originally published in Great Britain under the title *The Detling Murders*.

LIBRARY OF CONGRESS CATALOGING IN PUBLICATION DATA
    Symons, Julian, 1912–
      The Detling secret.
      I. Title.
    PR6037.Y5D4   1983   823'.912   82-8591
    ISBN 0-670-27063-6

Printed in the United States of America

To Christine Symons

The mysterious stranger arrives. Is his roaring meant
To tell us that a Daniel's come to judgement?

Contents

PRELUDE

1 *The Proposal*

'Not to be thought of,' Sir Arthur Detling said. 'I tell you it is not to be thought of, and there's an end of it.'

'But, my dear, Dolly *is* thinking of it.'

'Then she must think again. I hope you have not encouraged her, Matilda.'

'You know as well as I that nothing can influence Dolly once she has made up her mind.'

'Stuff and nonsense. I've hardly heard of the man.'

'He has been to dinner here. And to more than one of my At Homes.'

'It seems to me sometimes that you keep open house for half the rag, tag and bobtail in London. As for being here at dinner, I don't remember it.'

'Of course you do. It was quite a political evening, we balanced the numbers perfectly, three Unionist members and three Liberals, all of them interested in the Irish question. You must remember.'

'I remember a lot of stupid talk.'

'Mr Ross was one of the Liberals.'

'Then I make no doubt he gave us more than his share of it. Not that I have prejudices, I should make no bones about sitting down at table with a Hottentot. That does not mean I should be prepared to let him marry my daughter.'

Matilda Detling sighed, put her hands together, looked down at the carpet and forbore to say that Mr Ross was not a Hottentot. They were sitting in the study of their comfortable town house off Belgrave Square. "Town house" is almost a misnomer, for although they had a pleasant enough residence in Kent, it was left to the servants for all but a few weeks every year. She had known there would be trouble because of Mr Ross's politics, for Sir Arthur was a strong Tory, who believed that the country had been ruined by the passing of the Reform Bill sixty years ago. He spent a good deal of time at the Conservative Club, where he found many companions with similar views. He liked giving and attending dinner parties, however much he might complain about the company, and enjoyed hearing the latest gossip, discussing who was in favour this week and might be out next. Matilda for her part, although she could not aspire to a salon, gave literary and artistic evenings to which the giants of the moment were invited, and sometimes came, along with many who were certainly not giants and perhaps hardly reached the stature of pygmies.

The Detlings were a handsome couple. Sir Arthur, whose baronetage went back nearly three centuries to a piratical capture of two Spanish merchantmen for which his ancestor Roderick had been honoured by Queen Elizabeth, had at sixty a good head of grey hair, a powerful nose, firm and regular features. The head of a Roman Emperor, somebody had said when he was young. The effect was somewhat spoiled by the fact that this fine head and massive trunk were mounted on very short legs, so that he looked impressive while seated but slightly absurd when he stood up. Matilda was not a tall woman, but she was almost of a height with her husband. She had dark hair which was coiled in braids, a delicate heart-shaped face, and a figure on which she was often complimented. Perhaps the fact that their family numbered no more than three had helped her to retain an hour-glass shape. There were a son and two daughters. Roderick, the eldest, was married, well in one way and not so well in another. His wife Gertrude was the daughter of a man highly regarded in the

City as the promoter of many companies. Joseph Blader was evidently a rich man, and that was the good side of the marriage. On the other hand he was nobody, just a City financier, and that was the bad side of it. The Dorothy they had been discussing and her younger sister Eleanor were unmarried.

The man who wanted to marry Dorothy, or Dolly as they had called her since she was a child, was named Bernard Ross. Far from being a Hottentot he was unusually good-looking, with an olive skin and dark lustrous eyes. He was a Member for a Midlands constituency, and was often on his feet in the House, where he was spoken of as a coming man. Matilda asked what was wrong about Mr Ross, and the reply acknowledged what they both knew, that he remembered the young man perfectly well.

'Wrong, I don't know that there's anything *wrong*. He won't do for Dolly, that's all.'

In a gentle, hesitant way Matilda could be persistent. 'But there must be a reason why he won't do, my dear. I know little of such things, but I hear that his speech a week or two ago on the Irish question was impressive.'

'That's not the point, not the point at all. I daresay he can make a pretty speech and say sweet nothings, but who is he? Where does he come from, what's his family? He doesn't look like an Englishman, I can tell you that.'

'Many of the greatest writers have been foreign, like Goethe and Voltaire. And then, Sir Arthur, you have no prejudices, you have just said so.'

He flinched a little at that, for his wife only called him 'Sir Arthur' when she was displeased. But still the matter was important, and he continued.

'I've heard a little about the fellow, and I'll tell you what

11

people say. They ask what he lives on. As far as I know he. hasn't a penny to bless himself with. And then why doesn't he come to me himself like a man, instead of speaking to Dolly? The upshot is I've not been told a word about it until now, not a word. Is that a right kind of behaviour? It wouldn't have done when I was a young man, I can tell you that.'

'Oh dear. I see that I should not have spoken, but after what Dolly said to me –'

'And just what did she say? I am still waiting to hear.'

'Why, that Mr Ross had proposed marriage, and that she had accepted him.'

'Indeed. *Indeed.*' He got up and strutted indignantly about the room. 'It didn't occur to him that he should speak to Dolly's father first?'

'I suppose he did not think you would be so old fashioned. Neither did I. I thought you would be pleased. You had better speak to Dolly yourself.'

He said that he would, and with that she left him. He rang the bell, and asked that his elder daughter should be told that he wished to speak to her. He did not look forward to the interview, for he was slightly in awe of Dorothy. For one thing she was a tall girl, distinctly taller than her father, and then there was something imperious about her. She could be forceful in a way that he considered almost unladylike. Sir Arthur liked to think that he was forceful too, and certainly he sometimes used strong language about political matters, but he knew that his bark was not matched by any accompanying bite. Dorothy, however, could inflict lasting wounds upon occasion, and did not respect her elders as he thought a well-brought-up girl should. Yet Ross seemed to him so unsuitable as a son-in-law that he was determined to talk to her.

Dolly came in, and sat down with composure. She was dark

haired like her mother and had her father's regular features, but the total effect was of strength rather than beauty. He cleared his throat.

'Your mother tells me that Mr Ross has proposed marriage to you. I presume that's the Ross who sits in the talking shop?'

'Mr Ross is in Parliament, yes.'

'It won't do, you know.' She made no reply to this, and only raised her shapely but thick eyebrows, apparently waiting for him to go on. He did so, a little lamely. 'For one thing, he should have come to me first.'

'Really? And supposing you had said yes but then I had refused him, wouldn't he have looked foolish? I am sure Bernard has written you a letter, and that it will arrive by today's post. I am sorry that you heard the news from mamma, but surely that is not important?'

'It's not the most important thing, no. The thing is, it won't do.'

'Father, why do you say that? Bernard has proposed and I have accepted him. Is there something I should know about him? It cannot be anything very bad, surely, for it was in this house that I first met him.'

'As I told your mother, all kinds of people come to her affairs. Why shouldn't he marry you, you ask? Well now, I don't doubt that when he proposed he said he loved you, got down on his knees and all that –'

'We are not in the days of your youth, father, we are in the nineties. Of course Bernard did not go down on his knees.'

'In my youth it was thought bad manners to interrupt your elders, but I suppose all that's gone by the board, any sort of behaviour is accepted nowadays. You ask what my objections are? I want to know where he comes from and how he's going to support you, that's the sum of them. Did he enlighten you on those points?'

13

'Bernard has told me that he was born in this country, but that his family emigrated to America at a time he was too young to remember. His parents both died when he was young, and he was brought up by an uncle in what I believe is called the mid-West. They were not people of our kind. I understand his father was a small farmer, or something of the sort. I thought it manly of him to tell me all that, I respected him for his frankness. We are democratic enough now to understand that a man's background is of no importance.'

'On the contrary, it's the most important thing about him, tells you who he is. Any Tom, Dick or Harry can become a Member of Parliament nowadays. No need for any background, he could be the son of a butcher. Or a traitor to the country like those Irishmen asking for what they call Home Rule. It's not the way things used to be, I can tell you.'

'All this has nothing to do with Bernard.'

'It does indeed. You are telling me he has no family at all.'

'There is a brother who has done well in business, but he is in America. Bernard came over here ten years ago or more.'

'And how does he intend to support you?'

For the first time Dolly lost a little of her sureness. 'He knows people in the City. I understand he acts as an adviser to Mr Blader in some matters.'

'That may amount to nothing at all. It sounds to me as if he expects a good settlement with you, and proposes to live off it while he makes a career in politics. Let me tell you that even if I were in a position to consider such a thing, which I am not, I should not do it. There is your sister, remember. You don't seem to think of her.'

'Oh father, really.' She sighed. 'Why not wait until you receive the letter?'

A little after that she retired, and he felt he had done pretty well. It was untrue that he could not afford to give both his daughters a decent settlement, but he saw no reason why Ross should build a political career – and as a Liberal, of all things – while using him as a backer. His daughter's talk about background being of no importance had annoyed him. He believed that good blood came out in men as in horses. Only a headstrong, opinionated girl could indulge in that nonsense about being democratic, when the plain fact was that a penniless orphan was looking for money and position by marrying her.

By the time he heard from Ross, Sir Arthur had worked himself into a passion which the letter did nothing to assuage. It would have been hard to find fault with the wording, which said simply that he had proposed to Dorothy and been accepted, and that he hoped her father would grant him an interview so that they might discuss details. But the tone of the whole thing infuriated him. Was it not the coolest insolence imaginable on the part of this penniless foreigner to take the whole thing for granted in that way? Borne on the wave of indignation, he made what seemed to him a devastating reply. It was in the third person:

Sir Arthur Detling has received Mr Ross's letter asking for his approval of Mr Ross's proposal of marriage to Miss Dorothy Detling, and requesting an interview for the purpose of "discussing details", as it is put. Since Sir Arthur is unable to approve the proposed match, however, it follows that there are no details to be discussed, and hence that such an interview would be a waste of Mr Ross's valuable time.

He was delighted with the letter, particularly with the final phrase, and sent it to the post before he could have second thoughts. He told his wife that he had received a letter and answered it, but did not mention that he had replied in the third person or tell her what he had said, and she assumed that

15

he had written making an appointment to see Mr Ross. Sir Arthur went off to the Conservative Club, feeling that he had done uncommonly well.

2 _The Acceptance_

'Father is positively ridiculous,' Dolly said to her sister. 'Ridiculous and insulting. Does he think we are living in the Dark Ages? I have a good mind to tell Bernard that I will marry him next week.'

'What a splendid idea. Will you ask him to get a special licence? But what you don't understand, Dolly, is that father _is_ still living in the Dark Ages, he has no idea of what goes on nowadays. I shall try to get him to let Charlie paint him. He is an antiquity and should be preserved.'

Both girls were modern in their views, although Dolly was serious minded while Nelly might have been called frivolous. For the past three years Dolly had worked for an organisation down in the East End that found jobs in households for errant girls. Nelly, who had shown great facility in drawing and painting from childhood, had been accepted as a student at the Slade School of Art. Her father had for some time refused to give his consent to this, but Matilda had made it so plain that he was robbing the world of a great woman painter, and Nelly had wept so profusely, that he had given way. Nelly had been at the Slade a year now, and saw a good deal of another student there named Charlie Bangs.

Dolly had no interest in jokes about her father. 'I don't mean to marry next week, of course not, but in these days it is no more than a formality for approval to be asked in any reasonable family. I shall marry Bernard whether father approves or not, have no doubt about that.'

'Are you very much in love with each other?'

Dolly considered the question. 'We shall suit each other,

that's the way in which I would put it. Everybody says Bernard
is a rising man, and you know I have always been interested in
public affairs.'

'Oh Dolly, you're so practical. Soup kitchens and sewers
and that kind of thing I do find so uninteresting.'

'And then I am twenty-five. It is time I was married.'

Eleanor, who was three years younger than her sister, understood the force of the last remark. Two or three eligible young
men had been interested in Dorothy, but their interest had
faded, in part perhaps because of her forceful style of conversation. The style was apparent when she sought, and with
some difficulty obtained, an interview with her father.

Sir Arthur had been told by Matilda that his letter had
surprised Bernard Ross and angered and upset his daughter.
He had come to think that his refusal should perhaps have
been expressed in a different form. He knew himself to be less
staunch in conversation than on paper, and the letter had been
an attempt to avoid personal discussion. He managed to avoid
seeing Dolly for nearly a week, leaving the house uncomfort-
ably early to deal with imaginary business affairs, eating lunch
and sometimes dinner at the Club, but in the end reality had to
be faced. There was a letter from Ross, one to which he really
could not take exception, in which the man said that he hoped
Sir Arthur would at least consent to see him. He delayed
answering this, but the atmosphere at home became so
strained that in the end he had to see Dolly. He had asked
Matilda to be in the room for protection, although of course he
would not have used the word. It was somehow a further
protection that they talked in the library. The presence of all
those calf-bound books on the shelves, the wisdom of the past
as they might be called, gave him a feeling of security. The first
thing Dolly said was that he had been avoiding her.

'Not at all. Nonsense. I have been very busy.'

'And to insult Bernard by sending a letter in the third person. Father, how could you?' He said something to the effect that no insult had been intended. 'And when he writes again – most courteously, he has shown me a copy of what he wrote – you do not even reply. Do you want to wreck my chance of happiness in life, father, is that your intention?'

'Politeness is the courtesy of princes,' Matilda said. She had a gift for getting well known quotations slightly wrong. 'I do think, my dear, that you have been rude to Mr Ross.'

Was it for this that he had asked his wife to be present? He felt the anger of all weak characters who know they have done something wrong, and thumped the top of his writing desk. 'I will not have you both going on like this. Dorothy, you know very well that my only concern is for your future. I don't wish you to have to bring up a family without a penny in the bank, is that unreasonable? I don't know what has come over you both, that I should be reproached for doing my best to look after my daughter's affairs. I told him I refused my permission, and that's that.'

His daughter asked what it was precisely that he complained about in relation to Bernard.

'I told you before that he should have come to me like a straight man, and said my family background is such and such, this is my present income, these are my prospects. He did nothing of the kind, no such thing.'

'He will do all of that, if you will only see him.'

'I have no wish to see him.'

'You must surely see, father, that a refusal to see him now would be an insult that he has done nothing to deserve.'

There was a good deal more of the same. In the end he agreed to see Ross, although he emphasised that an interview

19

would serve no purpose that could not be achieved just as well by correspondence. He wrote a short note asking Ross to name a day next week convenient to him, and received a reply by return.

Before this, however, he met his son Roderick at a club called the Oval Table. He had an uneasy feeling that news of his daughter's involement with a Liberal M.P., and not only a Liberal but one on the Radical side of that party, was getting round in the Conservative Club. People might make jokes, or sympathise with him, which would be worse. At the Oval Table there was no splendid tessellated floor as at the Conservative Club, no Ionic pillars or scagliola Corinthian columns. It was a modest place in an obscure street near Ludgate Circus. The company, which consisted mostly of men in and about the City, did not compare with that at the Conservative Club, but at least there would be no sidewise looks, or remarks passed behind the ·hand, such as he fancied he had seen there. Sir Arthur had been put up for the Oval Table by his son, and found that he did not mind the place. It was comfortable enough, and the chops and steaks were well cooked. Whist and other games were played for rather high stakes, but that did not matter to him. He was drinking coffee after lunch, and looking at *Punch*, when Roderick dropped into the armchair beside him and began to talk.

Roderick was of the same build as his father, with the same short legs and the same splendid head of hair, although his was black and not grey. His features were like a slightly blurred copy of Sir Arthur's, so that the effect was one of weakness. It did not belie the facts. Roderick enjoyed gambling, and had got himself into more than one scrape involving debts that his father had settled. All this, however, seemed to have ended since his marriage two years ago to Gertrude Blader. He had a job in the Home Office that was almost a sinecure, or at least allowed him to spend more time than his father thought proper as some sort of supernumerary in the Blader empire.

Roderick launched at once into the subject that his father had come to the Oval Table to avoid. 'I hear Dolly wants to marry Bernard Ross, but you're making a to-do about it.' Sir Arthur shifted uneasily. 'That's a lot of rot, you know. I don't know about his politics, but Ross is a good fellow. The governor thinks a lot of him.'

The governor was Joseph Blader. No doubt in financial circles Blader's opinion carried weight, but since it was favourable to Ross Sir Arthur had no wish to hear it. He asked in a far from welcoming tone what Blader knew about it.

'Why, just that Ross has worked in with him on two or three schemes, and he's uncommon quick in the uptake, so the governor says. You'd have to get up early in the morning to find anyone who'd be quicker in getting the meat out of a company prospectus, putting his finger on the point. He's got a future in business if he wants. That's what the governor says.'

Sir Arthur's irritation at being pestered in this way, in a place he had come to for the sake of peace, was profound. He responded only with a grunt. His son continued.

'Then I was talking to a chap the other night who knows a man who knows the Whips, and he said Ross might be in line for a place in the Irish Office. People think highly of him.'

To be instructed in this way by Roderick, who had no interest in or knowledge of politics, was more than his father could bear. 'I've no concern at all with what goes on in the talking shop. I think I know more about what's right for my daughter than you do.'

'I'm only telling you what I hear.'

'What you hear is of remarkably little importance in this

21

matter.' He put aside *Punch*, which had been spoiled for him, and got up to go.

'In any case, you know what Dolly's like. She always gets her way.'

Sir Arthur left his son with a curt goodbye, but on the way home he pondered what had been said, in particular those last words. It was true that Dolly had always showed great persistence, whether it was getting a pony in childhood, or working among the East End poor. He had tolerated what seemed to him this folly, because he knew that there was a craze in society for slumming, and it might be that her activities in the East End would lead to acquaintance with a worthy and eligible young man, although in fact that had not happened. And then he supposed that Blader must know what he was talking about when he spoke of Ross's financial astuteness, although the way in which it had been put was uncongenial. One way and another, his defences had to a certain extent been breached by the time he saw Bernard Ross.

Sir Arthur was old fashioned in the way of dress. He wore a morning coat during the day and changed into a tail coat for the evening, whether or not he was dining out. He knew that young men now went in for lounge coats, but still he did not care for Ross's lounge suit in a check design, with braided edges on the jacket lapels and pockets. He felt it showed a lack of seriousness to be wearing those clothes for such an interview.

He began in a manner finely intimidating. 'I believe, Mr Ross, that you have something to say to me.'

Bernard Ross sat with one leg crossed over another, at ease. He was certainly an extremely good-looking young man.

'I hoped I had already said it in my letter. I understand you feel I should have approached you first, and I'm sorry for that.

But still, what's been done is done. I proposed to Dorothy and she accepted me, and we both hope for your approval.'

'There's a form in these matters and it should be observed, although I daresay you don't think so.' Ross gave no sign either of assent or denial. 'I'm not an unreasonable man, nobody can say that. A father must look after his daughter, however.'

'You want to know my prospects? They are bright. We are in office, and I have every reason to expect a Government post in the next few months. You wish to know my past? It doesn't exist.'

'What's that? I don't understand you.'

'My father was a jobbing printer, who found it impossible to make a living here. He took his family to America when I was less than a year old, to try farming in Illinois at a little place called Gardville Grove. They had been there only twelve months when their farmhouse burned down as the result of a lamp being knocked over. They died in the fire, but my elder brother Jacob and I were saved. My uncle Ebenezer, who had emigrated some years earlier and had a prosperous fancy goods business in Chicago, brought us up. Jake stayed in the States and when I last heard of him was doing well, but we have been out of touch since I came back to the old country, and that was years ago, when I was twenty-one. I found work in my father's old occupation of printing. I rose quickly to be foreman of the printing works, and at the same time took a course of evening studies with a view to reading for the law. One of the lecturers was Mr Wandle the Member of Parliament, with whom I know you are acquainted, since we have both dined in your house. He took a generous interest in me from the first, and it was he who suggested that I should stand for Parliament. I did so, and was elected four years ago at the

23

age of twenty-seven.' The young man said all this with the utmost coolness. At the end he permitted himself a slight smile as he said, 'You will understand what I mean by saying that I have no past, but look forward with confidence to the future.'

Sir Arthur found himself rather at a loss. It was hardly possible, he felt, to go into great detail about the sad beginnings of this life story, nor to ask the name of the firm at which Ross had worked, as though he were requesting a reference from somebody applying for a job. He vaguely recalled Wandle, a man who could reel off statistics about infant mortality in Hoxton and the East End as though he were reading them from a book, and no doubt Wandle could tell him more. The frankness with which the story had been told was no doubt to the young man's credit. Yet there was something about the contrast between the tale of self-improvement and the casual ease, almost foppishness, of Ross's dress, that annoyed him. It was true also that he did not want his daughter to marry a man without family, a man who had been a foreman printer. And wasn't it a pretty piece of cheek – a slang use of the word of a kind he deprecated, but which did seem to fit the case – not to say a single word about money? Nevertheless, he felt that he would be putting himself in the wrong by approaching the question of money crudely. He gave a preliminary cough.

'A very pathetic story. One that does you credit. And Mr Wandle also.'

'I owe him more than I can say.'

'I hope your future will be as bright as you suggest. But there remains the question of how you will support a wife and family.'

Ross looked him directly in the eye. 'By my own efforts.'

'I am delighted to hear it, but that hardly answers my question.'

'And for a time, I hope, with your assistance.'

The effrontery of it fairly took Sir Arthur's breath away, yet this effect too was something which the young man who sat on the other side of the study seemed to have calculated. He uncrossed his legs now and leaned forward, hands on knees. His casualness had gone, replaced by an earnestness that was undoubtedly impressive.

'I think it right to be frank. I know very well that you can hardly welcome me as a son-in-law. What qualifications of birth or income do I have that can recommend me as a suitor for the daughter of one of the country's oldest families? None. But the fact is that Dorothy and I are going to get married. We are very firm about it, both of us, and there is nothing you can say that will change our minds. More than that, I know, I tell you I *know*, that I have a Parliamentary future. You cannot stop us, although Dorothy would hate to be on bad terms with her father, and so should I. It rests with you whether we begin our married life with the assurance that I can follow my political career free from immediate financial worry, or whether I must divert myself from politics, and be thinking always where the next hundred sovereigns are to come from that will keep me out of the hands of the moneylenders.'

Put like that, and Sir Arthur was uneasily aware that his wife and daughter would put it in some such form, it sounded as though he was doing his best to wreck a promising Parliamentary career. Yet why the devil should he be this fellow's financial backer? It was hardly possible to say that, but he was determined to learn something about Ross's financial resources, and saw no reason why he should mince his words.

'You talk as though you haven't a penny, but you keep a set of rooms, you go round and about, and that's not done without money. What d'ye have by the way of a regular income, eh? I think it's something I'm entitled to ask.'

Ross shrugged, as he did everything, gracefully. 'You are entitled to ask, of course. Whether I can reply to your satisfaction is another matter. I advise Mr Blader in relation to several of his enterprises. He is in the process of floating companies to exploit American and Canadian copper mines, and some of them are in areas of which I have particular knowledge. I travelled in Canada in my late teens. Like America it is a wonderful country, a land of opportunity. Of course, you know Mr Blader.'

'Yes, yes.' If America and Canada were so wonderful, why the devil didn't you stay there? he wondered. 'That's all very fine and large, but when your work in floating these companies, if that's what it's called, is done –'

'Then there will be other companies. Or perhaps one of Mr Blader's rivals will find himself in need of advice.'

Sir Arthur grunted. As a statement of a suitor's financial position, what he had been told was profoundly unsatisfactory, but company flotation was a closed world to him. He had acquaintances who lent their names in support of companies with names like Western Australian Gold Mines or Paraguayan Railways. Money was given for use of their names, and nobody criticised them for it. His own idea was that to be mixed up in such things was almost as low as being in trade, but his son had married Blader's daughter, and he knew that Roderick did some work or other for the financier. If something was right for his son, why should it be wrong for his son-in-law? He ended the interview abruptly, by saying that he would think about the matter and write in a day or two. Half an hour later he was beset by his wife and daughter, wanting to know what had been decided.

'Decided? I'll tell you what's been decided. Your precious

Mr Ross has got no family and no income.'

'You knew that already,' Dolly said. 'He has prospects.'

'And he expects me to provide both.' He knew that he was unfair in saying this, for Ross had stressed that they would get married, come what may.

'Providence will always provide,' Matilda murmured.

'And what is that supposed to mean?'

'There is no blessing so great as an action that brings joy to others.'

Sir Arthur raised his voice as he said that he would not be bothered and bullyragged. He would make up his own mind, and they would be told what he had decided. But in truth he knew that the decision was already taken. He could not stand up against Matilda and Dolly working in tandem, and would have to give way. Within a week the engagement notice appeared in *The Times*. And having given way he surrendered completely. They wanted to get married quickly? Very well, let the banns be published next week if that was possible. Dolly had set her heart on a house in Kensington, even though it would of necessity be the less fashionable part? By all means look for one and tell him the cost, why did the bride's father exist except as a bottomless well of money?

When three months was specified as the time to elapse between engagement and wedding, so that Dolly would be a July bride, he made no complaint about the period's indecent brevity, and when Roderick said that Bernard was one of the smartest chaps out and a bally good catch for Dolly, Sir Arthur did not reprove his son either for his slang or his levity. He had his doubts, but nobody seemed to share them, so he kept silent.

3 Getting Married

The party given by the Detlings to celebrate Dolly's engagement had the confusion typical of most things they undertook. It was not specified that this was the party's purpose, because Matilda thought that to put it in this way might upset her husband, and Dolly simply did not care. And then the guest list was much more mixed than is usual, including as it did politicians who were invited because they were known to the prospective groom, and some of the literary men and artists present at Matilda's At Homes, along with a number who had been invited simply for their social or political standing. Several City gentlemen were present, looking for the most part rather out of place, as though they would have been pleased to be back in their offices, engaged in the more congenial occupations of issuing prospectuses, selling shares, or whatever other mysterious occupations they followed.

It was hardly to be expected that Mr Gladstone would put in an appearance, for the Prime Minister was in his eighties, and attended such social occasions very rarely. The more important members of his Cabinet, like Mr Asquith and Lord Rosebery, were also absent. However, the Chief Secretary for Ireland, Mr Morley, was there along with quite a clutch of Irish members, some of whom were seen to be attacking the food and drink with a zest suggesting that they had been fasting in preparation for the occasion. As was customary with the Detlings there was little organisation, so that a musical recital given by one of Matilda's protégés named de Santis took place in one drawing room, while a couple of rooms away and within earshot a velvet-jacketed desperate-looking young poet

29

named Vyvyan Eglantine was declaiming his sonnet series *Songs of Desire and Rejection.* Matilda moved among the guests with her characteristic look of amiable uncertainty. Bernard Ross received congratulations, and repeated often that he was a very lucky man.

'I am tired of hearing people say that,' Dolly said. 'It is as though you had no merit of your own, but were a lucky angler who had landed a big fish.'

'That is just what a good many of them think.'

'Then they are stupid and vulgar. I don't find such thoughts at all amusing.'

'For most people to think the worst of others is as natural as it is to think the best of ourselves.'

'That sounds as if it might have come from one of Oscar Wilde's cynical plays. I don't care for cynicism, Bernard.'

'Then cynicism is bound to wither in the fire of your disapproval.'

'That sounds like Mr Wilde too, taken at second or third hand.'

'And there he is.'

The bulky form of the dramatist could be seen at the far end of the drawing room, bending smiling over the hand of his hostess. Matilda felt a flutter of delight, for although Oscar Wilde had a slightly dubious reputation his play, *A Woman of No Importance,* was being played at the Haymarket to general applause, and he was undoubtedly a literary lion. What other lion was there for him to meet? She introduced him to Mr Morley, and the Chief Secretary looked down his long thin nose and murmured some words of congratulations about the play, of which he had heard wonderful things. There was no comparable lion in the literary field, where most of the fry could only be described as small, but Mr Wilde seemed to know, or at least to be aware of, them all. He spoke to obscure Celtic poetasters of the beautiful melancholy he had found in their poems, and to unpopular novelists of the subtlety with which they had created characters intricate as a sea shell. Such an efflorescence of geniality surrounded him that those nearby seemed almost to glow in its warmth.

To Dolly and Bernard he said something about the union of beauty and intelligence that seemed to gain originality as he uttered it. Then he said directly to Bernard, 'I hear you promise to do wonderful things for my unhappy country.'

'I hope I may have the chance.'

'I am sure you must be given it, Mr Ross. I have followed your brilliant career with deep admiration, and know you have that gift of imagination which is valued above all others by the Irish temperament. Show my countrymen that you understand their longing for freedom and their genius for suffering, and they will greet you as a brother.'

With that he passed on, to tell a promising actress that he had in mind a play which would include a wonderful part for her, and at last to encounter the youthful Eglantine, who stood mute in a corner now that his reading had finished. The shape of those sonnets was perfect, Mr Wilde said, making shapes himself in the air with his large hands, they were perfect as the flower that now bore a poet's name. A brief quotation about sweet musk-rose and eglantine, and another about eglantine in the warm hedge, and Oscar Wilde was gone, perhaps to another party, leaving an impression of conceited dandyism among those who had not spoken to him, and of warmth and generosity in those who had. He had done more than anybody else could have done to make the party a success.

Sir Arthur had done no more than shake hands with Wilde when he arrived, noticing with distaste the soft warmth of the man's hand and his very evidently waved hair. His chief concern was to discover something more about Ross's political prospects, and he found general agreement that when the Grand Old Man retired as he must surely do in the next few months, Ross would be given a place in the Irish Office. He also found the chance to have a chat with Wandle. The member for South Greenwich was a heavy-faced man with muttonchop whiskers and steel-rimmed spectacles. He was dressed in rusty-looking evening clothes, and was surrounded by a smell of camphor, as though he – or perhaps only his clothes – had recently been taken out of a storage cupboard. Sir Arthur said that he had been told of Mr Wandle's kindness to the young man engaged to marry his daughter. Wandle replied, as was customary with him, as if addressing a public meeting.

'It is a pleasure always, as well as a duty, to give what help we can to those who have been born in a lower position in society than their merits warrant. I saw at once the talent of young Bernard Ross, and did what I could to assist him.'

'You met him when he was attending evening classes, I believe?'

'That is so. You know, I am sure, of the work in education being done by the School Boards among the London poor, and of the visits made to every house in every street. There could be no greater benefit to the people than general education of all the young, but unhappily this is not always understood by their parents. Sometimes the Board visitors are met with abuse.'

There was nothing Sir Arthur disapproved of more strongly than the spread of education. What was the point of showing a farm labourer how to read and write? Or of teaching a servant girl the alphabet? It simply meant that they got ideas above their station. He said, 'That is surely not how you met

Bernard?' He found difficulty in uttering the Christian name.

'Quite true,' Mr Wandle said, as though conceding a point in debate. 'If memory serves, he attended a course in Municipal Government which I gave at Hoxton College. I was impressed by his grasp of the principles of the subject. It is sad but true that few people interest themselves in such matters.'

'And he was at that time a foreman in a printing works?'

'I believe so. I invited him to my home, and my good opinion of him was confirmed. It is among such people that we must look for the administrators of the future.'

The Lord help us if that is so, Sir Arthur thought but did not say. 'What about his background?'

'Oh, that is humble. His rise is an example of true worth.'

'No doubt, but what I had in mind was whether you knew anything of his parents or other relatives. Isn't there – well, damn it, has the man got *no* family?'

Something about the tone conveyed to Wandle that his answers were not altogether satisfactory. He removed and wiped his steel-rimmed spectacles, and the smell of camphor seemed to grow stronger.

'So far as I know, he has none in this country. In my view, that fact does him all the more credit.'

An attempt to buttonhole Blader had little more result. The City magnate was holding court to several people, Roderick among them, talking more loudly than he should have been about the ease with which fortunes could be made by investors who showed courage. When taken aside by his host, he showed no reluctance to discuss Ross.

'I've got the highest opinion of him, Sir Arthur, and I don't care who knows it. The only thing I'm sorry about is that he's gone into the political game instead of business. Of course, I don't doubt that he'll make a success of the other, but in

33

business he's got a real nose for what'll sell and the way to sell it.'

The fact that Blader made no attempt to conceal his commercial nature was perhaps commendable, but when Sir Arthur recalled that his son was married to this man's daughter, he despaired of the country's future.

'So you are likely to continue making use of his services?'

'I'll tell you my great principle in the world of commerce. I can sum it up in a word: usefulness. If you can be useful to me, why then, I must find a way of being useful to you. By helping you I help myself, and that's what makes the wheels go round and keeps us all prosperous. Young Roderick, now, is a good fellow, even though he's not too quick off the mark in telling an equity from a debenture, and of course it's no disadvantage that he's your son and my son-in-law. So what I say about usefulness applies there. Cuts both ways, if you take my meaning. Bernard now, if I had to sum Bernard up in a phrase, it would be that he's quick in the uptake.'

Had Blader taken more champagne on board than he should have done? Sir Arthur had rarely been made to wince so often during a short speech. Yet, however odious the financier's attitude might be, what he said could be called reassuring. Sir Arthur knew that several M.P.s used their parliamentary positions to further business careers, although he was hazy about how this was done. He had a chat with Mr Morley, and with the more genial Mr MacMurdo who was said to be the Chief Secretary's principal guide through the quicksand of Irish politics, but gathered no more than that they had a good opinion of Ross.

Dolly spent part of the evening talking to the politicians Bernard had said it would be useful for her to meet. Others might have found them dull, but she was keenly interested in such matters as the spread of educational opportunities and the relief of poverty, and was even able to listen without impatience to Mr Wandle. Later she found herself with Nelly and her sister-in-law Gertrude. The financier's daughter was a big, awkward young woman with a talent for wearing unsuitable clothes. On this evening she was dressed in an evening gown of electric blue satin with a very full puffed sleeve ending above the elbow. Her face was even more highly coloured than usual because of the effort she had made to confine her ample middle within the obligatory wasp waist. The effect, Nelly said afterwards, was to make Gertrude look like a costermonger's wife, but then Nelly did not know any costermonger's wives.

'Dereham Gardens,' Gertrude said, when she learned where the Rosses were to live. 'I don't think I know it.'

'That is not surprising. It is in an unfashionable part of Kensington.'

'But is that wise for Bernard? The governor says that you must have a good address, it's essential for success.'

'If that is the only criterion, then Bernard will obviously fail,' Dolly said coolly.

'Papa is not exactly mean, but he doesn't like actually spending money,' Nelly remarked. 'And then, as he keeps saying, he has me to think about. At least, that's what he says now. It would be a different tune if I said I was getting married next week.'

'Of course Bernard depends very much on the governor, or so I hear.'

'I have heard it put the other way, that your father finds his advice valuable,' Dolly replied. 'I see my mother beckoning. Excuse me.'

When she had gone, Gertrude said to Nelly, 'She seems very much on edge. I don't think she should mind my saying what I

35

did. I believe the things Bernard does for the governor are almost his only source of income. An M.P. gets no money, he is supposed to have private means, everybody knows that. I think one should face facts, don't you?'

'Yes. If a Member of Parliament proposes to me I shall ask for a signed declaration about the size of his private income as a preliminary before I think of accepting him.'

Gertrude fanned herself vigorously. 'You think it is clever to joke about such things. When the time comes you will find they are important.'

She left Eleanor, and later told her husband that Dolly took offence very easily, and that her younger sister was abominably pert. She added that Dolly put on airs of superiority that were unsuited to one who was going to live in some part of Kensington that nobody had ever heard of. Roderick, who always tried not to quarrel with his wife, made a suitably diplomatic reply.

Upon the whole, however, those chiefly involved were satisfied with the party. Sir Arthur had received some reassurance about his prospective son-in-law's future, Matilda felt that the appearance of Mr Morley and Mr Wilde, along with several sub-luminaries, meant that the evening had gone well, Bernard was pleased that so many politicians had been there, and Dolly was glad to have had the chance of talking to them, in some cases for the first time. As for Nelly, she danced a lot with Charlie Bangs, and flirted agreeably with one or two other young men.

The marriage at St George's, Hanover Square, was a quiet affair. Sir Arthur, having set up the young couple with a home, felt that he was not called upon to spend lavishly on the wedding, and of course the groom's lack of family connections meant that the guest list was very one-sided. Everything was done in proper form, however, and *The Times* reporter remarked particularly upon the bride's wedding dress of pale gold silk damask with an undergown of white satin. She was, of course, given away by her father, and the groom's best man was the genial Mr MacMurdo. The young couple departed for a honeymoon in Venice.

PART ONE

A DEATH IN LONDON

1 *Settling Down*

If Dolly had been asked what she expected of married life, she would have been likely to reply with a list of negatives. It was not fluff and orange blossom and sweet whispers in dark corners, it was not giving or attending At Homes and tea parties, it was not running a household or having children, although all those things played a part in it. If she had been forced to define what she expected in positive terms, she might have said that a wife should be a partner in her husband's career, and that she would wish to be such a partner. She was a modern woman, quite capable of reading a Committee report or studying a Blue Book. She was aware that she knew much more about social affairs than most of her sex, and saw herself as combining the roles of secretary and adviser to her husband. Venice was beautiful and romantic, all those Titians and Tintorettos and the other paintings in the churches were no doubt very fine, and Bernard could not have been more loving and attentive, but she had a frequent feeling that it was all unreal, and at times was impatient to get back to London and resume the proper business of living.

After a few weeks of life in Dereham Gardens, however, she had to admit to herself that things were not in all ways as she had expected. They had given and attended parties, and she had told her family as a matter of course that she was ecstatically happy, but that was not entirely true. The trouble, in a word, was Bernard. Not Bernard as a lover – as a modern young woman she had known more or less what to expect about that side of married life – but Bernard as a politician. After their first meeting he had taken her to art exhibitions and concerts, but

41

what she chiefly valued was admission to the life of politics. She had taken tea on the terrace at the House, talked to some of the other Members, and of course had been in the gallery to hear him speak.

She was much impressed by his speeches. He talked about Ireland, and said that there should be an Irish Parliament with powers of its own, although they would be limited by an English Viceroy. The constabulary must remain for the present under the Viceroy's control, and so must everything relating to Irish trade, but other domestic affairs would be handled by the Irish themselves. Similar things had been said by other Liberals, but Bernard Ross put them with such easy grace and style, in such perfectly-formed phrases uttered with no more than the merest glance at his notes, that the matter perhaps seemed more original than it was. She felt the hum of approval in the Chamber, noticed the friendly nods on the Front Bench, and agreed with the morning papers that referred to Mr Ross as a rising star.

The Irish question was the heart of Parliament that year. Mr Gladstone was determined to drive through a Home Rule Bill before his retirement, and the session which had begun at the end of January continued, with only a brief recess at Easter, through the whole of the summer, and showed no sign of ending, as the Tory opposition fought the Bill clause by clause. Reputations were to be made in these Irish debates, and she knew her husband must be aware of it. Surely, then, a politician worth his salt should be reading everything he could about his special subject, talking to the Irish Members and making allies among them, meeting some of those who regarded any talk of Home Rule as a betrayal of their hopes for a united Ireland, and in general preparing the ground for his own advancement? And should he not also be talking to his wife about such matters?

Bernard, however, seemed to take it all with a casualness of which she could not approve. The great Liberal club was the Reform, and certainly he often went there, but when she asked how his time had been spent he would say as often as not that he had been playing billiards. Apart from that, he went more often than she cared for to Blader's place in the City, where he was apparently concerned with the launching of a new company called North Canadian Goldfields.

With Dolly, to think was to speak in such matters, and she spoke one evening after dinner when they sat in the drawing room over-looking the central gardens.

'I see in the paper that it says the Fenians in America have sent new agents to stir up trouble in Ireland. Do you suppose Mr Morley is aware of that?'

Her husband was bending over a jigsaw, a scene from the Queen's Golden Jubilee. His liking for jigsaws, and indeed for any trivial thing that occupied his hands, had been unknown to her before their marriage. 'I should be surprised if he is not.'

'Does he know their names, do you think? Do *you* know their names?'

'Why no, my dear. Those are matters that may concern Scotland Yard, but they have nothing to do with me.'

'I should have thought they would concern anybody who wished for Ireland to be properly governed. We all know that when Mr Parnell died the Irish movement was left without a leader, and since then I have read about half-a-dozen groups wanting different things, some asking for Home Rule, others saying they must be free of any connection with Britain, others saying that Home Rule is nothing without a Land Bill. I wonder what you think about that, which group you think the Government should try to deal with. You never talk to me about politics.'

'Do I not?' He put away the jigsaw, came over and kissed her cheek. 'What a busy Dolly, to be worrying over such things. Do you really expect me to answer?'

'Is it an unreasonable question?'

'Not at all, so long as you accept a reasonable answer. Mr Gladstone's Government is in favour of Home Rule for Ireland, for the Irish to have their own Parliament sitting in Dublin. I am a member of Mr Gladstone's Liberal Party. I support Home Rule for Ireland.'

'That's no answer. You speak as if you had no personal opinion at all.'

'I don't see what more you expect. If I get an appointment under Morley, I shall do my best to carry out Government policy.'

'But I should have thought you would be in touch with people representing – oh, the Sinn Fein movement and this new group that call themselves the Gaelic League, and others. I should have expected them to be writing to you, and coming to see you.'

'Some of them do write. You will have seen letters with an Irish postmark. But you exaggerate my importance. I have no position, I am no more than a Member who has made a few speeches that people have been kind enough to praise. As to where I stand on the Irish question, I shall stand wherever I find it most comfortable to put my feet. You know that complaints are made about our revered leader, the Grand Old Man himself, to the effect that you can read some of his statements upon important issues upside down or right way up, and be no wiser whichever way you choose. Surely Mr Gladstone cannot be a bad model? And surely these are unusual matters for a young lady so recently married to puzzle her head about?'

'Bernard, I consent to being called Dolly because I have

44

been given the name ever since I was a child, but please don't try to treat me like a doll. I am interested in what you say and do, and you will get candour from me whether you like it or not. I think you spend too much time dancing attendance on Mr Blader, too little on your political career.'

'And if I were to criticise you, which of course I should never dream of doing, I should say that you might spend more time rebuking cook for burning the chops as she did the night before last, and sound less as though you wanted to be the first woman to enter Parliament. But there's no need to argue. Shall I give up this stupid jigsaw?' He swept it off the table on to the carpet. 'Shall we dance?' He pulled her to her feet and whirled around the room with her. 'Shall we ask your father and mother to dine and invite half-a-dozen of the most rabid Irish Members with them, so that your father may disapprove of me even more than he does?'

One of the things that Dolly liked most about her husband was that he made her laugh. She remained determined, however, that she would play some part in his political life.

2 *Two Young Gamblers*

Roderick's job in the Home Office was not an arduous one. He was a junior principal in a branch of the Department of Prison Services concerned with the condition of prisoners, their food, discipline and general well-being. This consisted in practice of exchanging minutes with other sections of the prison service about half-yearly reports made by prison Governors, something that occupied him upon an average no more than an hour a day.

The Home Office was a comfortable place in which to have a position. It was said that the Home Secretary could not recognise more than half of his staff, and there were some who interpreted the office hours of 11 to 5 so liberally that they came in at midday and left immediately after lunch. If the previous evening had been particularly strenuous, they did not come in at all. Roderick put in an appearance every day, but sometimes left at lunch time. On other days he spent a good deal of time with Paul Patterwick, who worked in a branch of the Home Office that had no separate existence on paper, but was known unofficially as the Irish Section. It dealt exclusively with Irish terrorism, and had worked with Scotland Yard in combating the attempts a few years earlier to blow up several public buildings, including the Houses of Parliament. Paul, whose job it was to keep a file on every known member or sympathiser with every Irish group, was the son of a Judge known colloquially as Patterwick the Hangman, and was in appearance so pale and colourless as to be almost an albino. He had only two passions in life, one for the proper keeping and cross-referencing of his files, and the other for gambling.

Roderick often sat with his feet up in Paul's dusty little room, wondering at the pleasure he took in identifying Peter Boyle, a member of the Band of Bold Irish Brothers, as identical with Paddy Bain of the Irish Republican Brotherhood.

However, it was gambling that joined the two young men, and they often spent long lunch hours at the Burlingham Club. The Burlingham offered no Club facilities, although you had to pay an entrance fee. There was a room at the front where you could get a chop or a steak, although most people ate savouries like Welsh rarebit, Scotch woodcock, or angels on horseback, which were served in slices and often eaten standing up while watching the play in the main room. The Burlingham was hardly Crockford's and all sorts of men came in there, including some very sharp customers. On this October day, however, Paul positively refused to go in and play, saying he had lost too much money recently.

'It's your own fault. Roulette's a mug's game, the advantage is always with the bank. If you watch the cards at vingt-et-un, you can't lose.'

'You must have lost as much as me or more.' Roderick did not deny it. 'You play. I'll watch you.'

Roderick shook his head. 'It would be bad luck. Besides, I'm down a lot myself. I should give it up.'

They ate their chops in the outer room, looking miserably at those who went inside, and even more so at the few who came out, hat on back of head, pocketing their winnings.

'If you're worrying about old Chailey, you needn't,' Paul said. 'He'll let you go on playing, providing you pay something off. Besides, you can't be into him for all that much.' Chailey was the owner of the Burlingham.

'It isn't only Chailey. I've had a deuced bad run lately. I suppose you can't manage any tin?'

Paul shook his head rapidly, his almost colourless lashes going up and down. 'Very short myself. Won't your father cough up? Or Blader? They say he's worth millions, and you married his daughter? If not, then it will have to be old Hagen. He'll do anything for you if you've got expectations.' Hagen was a moneylender known to them both.

'He has.'

'How d'you mean?'

'I signed notes for Hagen. Now they're due, and he wants his money.'

'I say, you *are* in a fix,' Paul said, with only slightly concealed pleasure. 'Worse than I am. Where have you been playing?'

'Here and there. I lost a bit at the Oval Table playing whist, and then I sometimes spend an hour or two here before going home. Marriage isn't a picnic, Gertrude can be a Tartar. You're better off not getting spliced.' Paul nodded, his feeling of well-being increased. Roderick ordered Welsh rarebit, and went on gloomily. 'My sister Dolly got married, you know, to that fellow Ross. What do you know about him?'

'Not much. He's been mentioned once or twice in letters from agents in the States. Some of the Fenians think he may favour them. They'd like to know where he stands.'

'I don't know what he does for money. Of course, he's in the governor's pocket. That's Blader, you know, we all call him that. Wish I was in his pocket too.' His noble Roman head was cast down in gloom. 'Think I'll sit down for a minute or two at the table. My luck might be in.'

He did so, but either his luck was out, or he did not follow his own advice and count the cards. Either way, he lost.

3   *An Evening in Howland Street*

When Nelly had insisted that she wanted to study art she had really meant that she wanted to know artists, and she had gone to the Slade rather than the Royal Academy schools because she had thought that at the Slade both teachers and students would be bohemian rebels. It was a shock to find herself on arrival put into the Antique Room and set to make sketches of Greek and Roman sculpture, rather than being allowed to draw from the life. She survived some weeks of this, saying to anybody interested that she thought she would die of boredom, but when she was allowed into the Life Class it was with a shock of a different kind that she saw a woman model seated on the dais completely naked.

She was so embarrassed that she was unable to do more than make the merest sidewise sketch of the model showing the outline of one breast, but the other students took the nakedness so much as a matter of course that within a week she also thought nothing of it. However, a strict discipline was kept at the Slade. The sexes sat apart from each other in the Life Class, separated by a gap in the middle of the room, and they were not encouraged to converse outside the class room. Two students, male and female, seen chatting in a corridor, were told by the professor in charge that the Slade was an art school, not a matrimonial agency.

Nevertheless, outside the school the students did mingle, and some even had studios, or rooms that served as studios, in the area off Gower Street where the Slade was situated, part of the University College quadrangle. Nelly met other students, and in particular she met Charlie Bangs.

Charlie was the son of an Irish solicitor, and had curly fair hair, an ingenuous smile, and a voice that was softly Irish without any kind of brogue. At school in Dublin he had shown such facility in drawing that his parents accepted without question his desire to go to art school. He had been in Paris for a few months, and came from there to the Slade. One day when Nelly and Charlie left the Life Class he handed her a drawing he had made of her from across the room. It showed her sitting on one of the wooden donkeys, pencil in hand, hair coming down over her forehead, face intent on the model. The drawing made her profile look finer and more delicate than it had ever seemed in a photograph. He had said carelessly that she could keep it if she liked, and that afternoon invited her round to his studio.

'It's perfectly all right,' he said when she hesitated. 'Half a dozen other people will be there. My old landlady feeds the starving artists with tea and cakes.'

The studio was a room in Warren Street, and had no right to the name except that it contained a large window, but Mrs Cable the landlady was real enough, and so were her Chelsea buns and Eccles cakes. She was a widow in her sixties who wore a bright golden wig. Her husband had been a painter, some of his pictures had been shown at the Royal Academy, and she liked nothing more than to be among young people and to talk about her husband and his painting. As for the half-dozen people, that number doubled as some who lived nearby drifted in, were given mugs of tea from the great pot that stood on the hob, and sat on chairs, cushions, the floor, anywhere they could find. Most of them were Slade students, others artists who lived in the neighbourhood, and the talk was all about art, about the need to get away from the fashionable painters like Frith and Alma-Tadema who were mere illustrators, and to draw like Aubrey Beardsley, paint like Whistler.

Nelly had never known people talk so much, nor had she ever met girls and young men prepared to sit casually on the floor. She listened, she was charmed, she returned. She began to think she was in love with Charlie Bangs.

One of those who ate Mrs Cable's buns and drank her tea was Eustace Settleby, a squat man with bad teeth and a face like a toad. Eustace was not a student but a man in his thirties, and a painter who gloried in his lack of success, which proved to him the corruption and stupidity of those who, as he called it, ran the world of art. He was opposed, like many of the Slade students, to the Royal Academicians, but he was equally contemptuous of the incessant copying, as he called it, that went on at the Slade. Whistler? If you liked little miniatures he was as good as anybody else. Nelly thought Settleby mean and jealous, and said so to Charlie, who laughed.

'You shouldn't take Eustace so seriously, he doesn't mean all he says. At least he's unusual, you must admit that.'

'I suppose so. What are his own paintings like? Are they so wonderful that he's entitled to sneer at other people?'

Charlie laughed again, and said that she could see for herself, Eustace was giving a party later in the week, and everybody was invited.

'I thought he was so poor.'

'I believe he gets remittances sometimes. Anyway, he has enough money to give a party. Perhaps he's borrowed it.'

Eustace Settleby's studio was on the top floor of a house in Howland Street, off Tottenham Court Road, and it was a room with a large skylight. One end was curtained off, no doubt concealing a bed and wash basin, and the rest of it was extremely dirty and untidy. Several of Eustace's canvases were on the walls. Nelly had never seen anything like them. They seemed to her no more than swirls of jarring bright colours, bitter reds, acid yellows, angry greens and purples, among which distorted faces and figures could be glimpsed. Another canvas stood on an easel, and in this she recognised through a criss-crossing of green and red lines the outlines of a window, a door, a figure, a chair. The painter stood beside her as she looked at the pictures on the walls.

'And what does the middle class miss have to say about them? Not quite the kind of thing to please the gentlemen at the Slade, I'm afraid.' A wheezing, rusty laugh seemed to have been squeezed out of his squat body.

'They are very vivid.'

'Is that the best you can find to say?' He thumped a long deal table piled with tubes of paint, rags, aprons, dirty glasses and empty bottles. 'Who's the greatest English artist of this century, eh? I'll tell you, Turner, Joseph William Mallord Turner. Little man, Turner, like me. Turner can't paint, they say, Settleby can't paint. All wrong. What you see in those paintings isn't Academy stuff, it's genius. Understand that, genius.' He was close to her. His breath smelt strongly of alcohol.

'Now, Eustace, that's no way at all to talk to Nelly,' Charlie said mildly. 'She said your paintings are vivid, and isn't that the truth? We're all friends here, I hope.'

'As long as it's understood,' Settleby said. 'Turner and Settleby, yes. The rest is rubbish, a lot of cliques scratching each other's backs. Or backsides. Have a drink.'

He waved a hand to a corner of the studio. There stood four large galvanised iron buckets filled with chunks of ice which surrounded several bottles of champagne. Charlie made his way across the room, and returned with glasses of champagne. Nelly caught sight of herself in a cracked mirror, loose smock-like dress, hair parted in the centre and hanging down, and thought that she was the prettiest girl there, even though she was not the best artist. That was undoubtedly Jenny Richards, another Slade student, whose drawings on religious themes were highly praised by everybody. Jenny had beautiful large dark eyes which she enhanced with kohl, but apart from that was really rather ugly. Was it better to be the prettiest girl or the best artist? Nelly knew which she preferred.

'I'm sorry,' Charlie said. 'Eustace was very rude. He often is.'

'It doesn't matter.' At this moment she was prepared to accept anything that was said, anything that happened. To be in this dingy room, full of dust and dirt, to see champagne bottles placed in buckets that at home would have been used for kitchen rubbish, to drink the sparkling wine from what looked like a toothglass by no means clean – all this was so wonderfully free and easy, so unlike the constriction of life in Belgravia, that she had hardly noticed what Eustace said. This, surely, was the perfect image of the bohemian life. She turned to her companion. 'Oh, Charlie, isn't it wonderful?'

'What baffles me is how Eustace comes to be so flush.' He had brought a bottle with him, and refilled their glasses. 'Hallo, Mrs Settleby, will you have some champagne?'

'Why not?' Mrs Settleby had a long horse face with lank hair drooping on either side of it. She seemed familiar yet Nelly could not remember meeting her, until she realised suddenly that this was one of the models in the Life Class, where she was called only Laura. No doubt she was the woman in the easel picture.

'I don't know where it comes from, at our parties it's usually just a glass of beer. Settleby, where did you get the ready?' She had raised her voice to ask the question, and the effect was like that of a bird screeching.

'Where do you think? I sold a picture.' There was a murmur

in the room, a sound that might have been laughter. 'You think that's impossible, you think nobody wants to buy a Settleby? Was it you laughing, you cow?' The squat body moved menacingly across to Laura. 'What do you know about art?'

'If standing up for hours in front of a crowd of bleeding students means anything, I know a lot. What's the matter with you, they're all pleased you've sold one of your masterpieces, or anyway they're pleased to drink your fizz. I wasn't laughing, Settleby, I know you're a genius.'

She put an arm round the painter and kissed him. There was another murmur, this time of approval, and people began to talk again. Settleby, released from Laura's embrace, looked round slowly, and again moved towards Nelly.

'This is a street of artists, painters, poets. You know who lived next door here in Howland Street a few years ago? Verlaine and Rimbaud. You know who they were? Of course you don't. Greatest French poet, Verlaine. Ugly like me, a great poet. Rimbaud, Arthur Rimbaud, great poet too, only eighteen years old. Verlaine's boy, you know what I mean? Middle class miss know what I mean?'

'Settleby, you just stop talking like that. It's the drink,' Laura said as she led him away. 'It makes him argumentative.'

Charlie Bangs said earnestly, 'I'm extremely sorry, I don't know why Eustace should pick on you like this. Perhaps you would like me to take you home.'

'Oh *no*. What I should like, Charlie, is another glass of champagne.'

She had that glass, and another, and after that she did not bother to count. She talked to Jenny Richards, and then to a student named Ambrose something or other, of whom she had always stood in awe because he seemed to know so much.

They discussed questions like whether art had a meaning or was just a matter of putting beautiful things on canvas, and she surprised herself by her own eloquence. Time passed, Laura appeared with hot meat pies which came from a pastrycook round the corner and which they ate with their fingers, and then a little or perhaps a lot later a tall piratical figure appeared in the doorway, wearing a great black hat and with gold rings in his ears.

She had seen him from a distance and knew that this was Christopher Grant, the student who had been called by Professor Tonks the greatest draughtsman since Michelangelo. He came in, embraced Laura, slapped Eustace on the back, kissed Jenny Richards's hand, drained a glass of champagne, and then drank another almost as quickly. She did not dare to speak to the great man, but heard him suggest that they should go round and finish the evening in the Anarchist Club.

At this Charlie took alarm, and said that he really must take her home. She rejected the idea.

'But Nelly, I don't think you should go to such a place.'

'And why not? Anarchists believe in *freedom*.' She flung her arms wide. 'And I know about those French poets too, I mean about what they did. I'm not a fool. You go home if you wish.'

Christopher, across the room, called out 'I believe in freedom too,' and raised his glass to her. Charlie said sulkily that if she wanted to visit the Anarchist Club, then of course he would go there too.

In fact the Club, which was no more than a few minutes' walk away, was a little disappointing. There were several dark bearded figures who talked to each other in a language said by Christopher Grant to be Spanish, but most of them were playing chess. She heard no talk of revolution, although there were men sitting at small marble-topped tables drinking lemon tea from glasses, and looking at foreign newspapers. Christopher pointed out an ordinary looking old lady who was, he said, Louise Michel. Nelly had never heard of Louise Michel, and said so.

'She fought on the barricades in the days of the Commune. They called her the Red Virgin.'

She stared. 'But I wasn't born then. Or I was only a baby.'

✓ 'So was I,' Christopher said, and roared with laughter. He whispered into her ear, 'You are the most beautiful girl here,' but a moment afterwards he waved to a man at the other side of the room, and went over to join him without a word of apology. Charlie was at the counter ordering lemon tea, so that she was left alone. Behind her she heard voices speaking English, and turned to see Eustace talking to three men she had not seen before. Eustace approached her, swaying a little. When he spoke, she noticed the blurring of his sibilants.

'This is the middle class miss I was talking about,' he said. 'Whatever else art is, I said to her, it's not middle class, but still she says she wants to be an artist.'

The men stood silent, listening with apparent attention. They were commonplace-looking men, rather stodgily respectable in appearance, yet there was something unEnglish about the clothes they wore and about the wideawake hats two of them had on their heads. The third man had removed his bowler, and when he spoke she realised from the shortened vowels and the soft voice, a little like Charlie's, that he was Irish American.

'Our friend has drink taken. Ignore him. It's Miss Detling, I believe. May I introduce myself? My name is Paddy Devas, and these are my friends Mr O'Brien and Mr Flaherty.' The men in wideawakes made stiff little bows. 'I see a table across there. Will you come and sit with us for a minute or two?'

Over by the counter Charlie was engaged in conversation with Jenny Richards, the lemon tea apparently forgotten. She let herself be led over to one of the tables. She was conscious that the room was wavering as though she were seeing it through a heat haze, so that it was a comfort to feel a chair beneath her.

'It's your sister that's married to Mr Ross, the Member of Parliament, isn't that so?' Devas asked, and she said that was true. 'Now that's very interesting to us.'

'We'd like to talk to him,' said Mr O'Brien. She saw with fascination that his jaws moved rhythmically, even though he seemed not to be eating anything. Devas spoke again.

'The fact is, your brother-in-law's concerned with Irish matters, and as you'll have guessed by now since you're a clever young lady, so are we. We've come over from the States, and it would be a help to us if we could be talking to somebody who had the ear of the Government. Just a quiet talk, the kind that can harm nobody and may be a benefit to all. Now, if I write down the address where my friends and I are staying, would you be kind enough to pass it on to him? Then if he's inclined to get in touch, he can. I believe he'll know the name of Devas.'

The room was now quite certainly swaying a little, not an unpleasant sensation. Even the chair in which she sat seemed to be moving. When Eustace's voice spoke from behind her ear, she realised that he was holding her chair-back.

'Paddy's already acquainted with the family.'

Devas, unlike his companions, had lively, mobile features, which now showed anger. 'What the hell d'ye mean by that?'

'Just that it's a middle class family, that's all. Father may be Sir Somebody, but family's still middle class. Got all the money in the world, but all Philistines. I could give you –'

Devas stood up and roared, 'Shut your gob, Eustace Settleby, you're drunk.'

As though at a signal the other Irishmen were on their feet, and the one named O'Brien took Eustace by the collar. The painter may have been drunk, but he had sufficient agility to squirm out of O'Brien's grip and to land him a blow on the cheek. At that Flaherty caught Eustace round the waist and dragged him to the ground, knocking over one of the marble tables. There were shouts and screams, Laura appeared wielding an umbrella, with which she hit the Irishmen, Devas calmly pushed a piece of paper across to Nelly and said that he would be obliged if she would give it to her brother-in-law. Two previously unseen waiters began to drag the three struggling men towards the door, and Laura went with them, prodding O'Brien with the umbrella.

Then Charlie was there, pulling Nelly to her feet. She would have liked to stay in the Club and fall asleep, but still she let herself be pulled out into the street, and then into a passing cab. The last thing she saw was Eustace, his nose bloody, struggling with the two Irishmen, while Laura hovered round them. Devas was not to be seen.

Charlie was almost incoherent with regret at leaving her.

'Oh, Charlie, it was wonderful. Such nice people. Are parties always like this?'

'Not the ones I go to. Are you sure you weren't hurt?'

'Oh, no no no. Do you suppose that Mr Devas and those other men in the funny hats, do you suppose they're what people call terrorists? I liked Mr Devas. But why does Eustace hate me, why does he keep saying I'm middle class? Am I middle class, Charlie?'

'You're an angel.' Charlie kissed her, which was something he had done only once before.

'A middle class angel?' she asked, and then suddenly fell asleep.

When they got home he supported her to the front door, and told the footman that Miss Eleanor was unwell. Fortunately her father and mother were already asleep. The journey upstairs was managed without misadventure, and her hurriedly summoned lady's maid put her to bed.

4 *An Acquisition to the Family*

Dolly had by no means given up her social work. On Mondays, Wednesdays and Fridays she travelled to Aldgate by omnibus and railway, and then walked down to the pair of rooms in the Whitechapel Road that were the headquarters of the Association for the Assistance of Derelict Girls. She was never later than nine thirty but Mr Modkin, the Association's chairman, was always there before her.

Mr Modkin was a tall thin man with a huge Adam's apple, which moved up and down at great speed. He had all his clothes made by young people who were learning the craft of tailoring, so that they never fitted, and wore a stovepipe hat which he had bought by post and which was too large for him, so that it always perched dangerously on the back of his head. The Association tried to place derelict girls in positions as servants, and the rest of the staff consisted of a secretary named Mary Tracy, who worked full time, and several unpaid voluntary helpers like Dolly.

But what exactly was a derelict girl? Certainly one who was wandering the streets could be called derelict, but what about those living in houses where a family of eight or nine were together in a single room? Mr Modkin had said at first that all who came to them for help should be considered derelict, but this had unfortunate results. Girls who proved to be accomplished thieves were placed in houses where within a week they had run off with their mistress's purse, or stolen the silver. It was decided that the backgrounds of all girls must be investigated before they were placed in domestic service, and this was the function of the unpaid helpers.

On a particular Friday morning, three days after Nelly's party, Dolly arrived to find Mr Modkin talking to a small dark girl who had on a kind of purple sack, which must have been cut down from a dress of some quality, but was now extremely dirty. A smell like that of rotting vegetation surrounded her, but Mr Modkin seemed oblivious of it.

'Ah, Mrs Ross,' he said in his thin, fluting voice. 'How very fortunate that you are here. This is Lizzie, um, Lizzie Comstock, who has a home in, um, um –'

'Purchase Court,' Mary said from her desk, and made a face at Dolly.

'Purchase Court, just so. Lizzie has come to us because the family is unhappily too large to be adequately accommodated within the rather, um, circumscribed living space, isn't that so, Lizzie?'

The girl looked at him uncomprehendingly and said, 'My dad 'its me.'

'Dear me, yes.' Mr Modkin made a whistling noise of regret. 'Now, Mrs, um, Ross, may I pass Lizzie over to your, ah, care for the moment?'

Dolly approached Lizzie and said, 'Come along, Lizzie. The first thing is a wash. Then perhaps we can find you some new clothes.' At close range the smell more nearly resembled very strong cheese.

''Ere, what are you on abaht? Nobody told me abaht washing, they said if I came 'ere I'd get a job away from 'ome, that's all.'

The back room contained a wash basin and a gas ring. Dolly put on a kettle and looked at the girl's hair, which was full of nits. Before starting this work, she had hardly known such vermin existed, but now she took them for granted. With a good deal of protest from Lizzie the process of washing body and scrubbing head was carried out. Then she was given clean underwear and a blue and white dress from the storeroom at the back of the building, which was full of cast-offs contributed by bountiful ladies. The cheese smell proved to have emanated chiefly from the purple dress, which Dolly put aside to be burned. She took Lizzie to inspect herself in a glass.

'Gord, I look different,' she said. 'Where's me dress?'

'You won't be able to put it on again. It's worn out.'

'I want me dress.' Dolly took her back to Mr Modkin. 'She's bleedin' well pinched me dress.'

Mr Modkin whistled. 'If you are going into service, Lizzie, you will have to, um, modify your language. Mrs, um, Ross has provided you with new clothes which look, if I may say so, um, um –'

'Delightful,' Dolly said.

'Delightful, yes. Now, Lizzie, I hope we can place you in a suitable, um, situation with an employer. Your parents, however, are your, um, lawful guardians and it is a preliminary, um, condition that their consent must be obtained. Mrs, um, Ross will accompany you to visit them.'

'What the bleedin' 'ell's 'e on abaht?' the girl asked Dolly. She put her hand over her mouth. 'Sorry, it just slipped out.'

Purchase Court was among the network of courts and alleys which made up the worst part of Whitechapel. Most of the houses were wooden and dilapidated, and a standpipe at the end of each court provided the only water for drinking or washing. There were no outdoor privies, and indeed no room for them, because the houses stood side to side and back to back. A pit in the cellar was the only sanitation, with the result that a powerful stench of dung and urine struck the nostrils as soon as one entered a house. It was among these courts that, only a few years earlier, Jack the Ripper had carried out his murders, and although the Queen's edict that the lighting must be improved had been obeyed, the police patrolled here at night only in couples.

Dolly had been in one or two of the houses before, but could not refrain from putting a handkerchief to her nose as she went in. The smell lessened as they went up the stairs, but the house seemed to darken, and indeed this was so, for the little landing windows had been broken and stuffed with rags, so that no light came through. When Dolly asked what work Lizzie's father did, the girl stared at her, and then said he was sometimes down at the docks. 'Mostly, though, 'e's in the pub.'

On the top floor she pushed open a door. The scene within was now familiar to Dolly, and indeed this room was not so bad as many because the paper was still on the walls, and some attempt had been made to keep the place clean. There were two broken-down beds, on one of which a man was snoring, while a woman sat on the other, sewing in the light that came through a small unbroken window. Two boys and a girl, all younger than Lizzie and all very dirty, sat at a part-broken table, two sitting on chairs and the other on a packing case, playing a game which Dolly recognised as fivestones. And that was all. There was no gaslight, no means of cooking, no other furniture except more wooden boxes which served as a kind of chest-of-drawers for the family's few possessions. The woman put down her sewing, and looked questioningly at Lizzie.

'Ma, she's from rahnd the corner. She's going to get me a job. She took away me dress.' To her astonishment Dolly found that Lizzie was holding her hand. 'It was you as said I should do it, ma.'

'You're the charity,' the woman said.

'It's not a charity, but I hope we can place Lizzie in service.'

66

That was the form of words she had been told to use, a form that seemed ridiculous in that room and among these people. So did the next copybook phrase. 'But we need your agreement in writing. I have the form here.'

'I wanted it,' the woman said. 'You look ever so nice, Liz. Come here.' Lizzie went to her mother, who wept as they embraced. 'It's better for her, you see. Jim's all right with the others but he knocks her about, specially when he's on the drink. You know why it is, Liz, you understand?' Lizzie nodded. She did not cry. 'She's fourteen, though she don't look it. She's small for her age, but she'll grow with a bit of feeding up. Give me the paper.'

The man on the bed stirred. 'What will happen when he finds out what you've done?'

'Most likely he'll say good riddance, one less to feed, not that he does much feeding. There's little work to be had now down at the docks, and when there's nothing he goes on the drink.' Other visitors had told tales of angry fathers who had advanced with threats of violence if their children were taken away, but Dolly felt it to be her duty to ask whether the man shouldn't be woken. She saw Lizzie shrink at the suggestion. The woman said, 'No, you leave him to me, I'm used to his ways. You'll let me know how she's getting on, won't you, if I come round and ask?' She signed the paper.

'Of course we will. I'm sure Lizzie is a good girl and that she'll be very happy.' That also was a standard phrase, which Dolly knew to be far from true.

'Goodbye for now, Liz.' Another embrace, and then the woman wiped her eyes with her skirt. 'Say goodbye to your brothers and your sister.'

'Bye Tom, bye Billy, bye Dora.'

The children interrupted throwing their fivestones just long

enough to say goodbye, and then returned to the game. They
don't know what it means, Dolly thought in a despairing
moment, and neither does she. Then the smell of the house
assailed her again as they went down the stairs, and she
thought that any other existence must be better than this.

Purchase Court outside was dismal enough, but she felt on
coming out of the house as though she were breathing the fresh
air of Kent. As they left the house a man entering it said hallo
to Lizzie. He was a small man with a red nose, and Dolly
noticed him only because his clothes although shabby were
neat, and he wore a collar and tie. She asked Lizzie who it was.

'That's Fred. 'E's been in jail, 'e's ever so clever.' Dolly
forbore to say that it would have been more clever still to have
kept out of prison, and asked what he did. 'I dunno. Fred 'ad a
toff down to see 'im the other day, a real toff with a top 'at.
Shook 'ands with Fred just like they were friends. So you ain't
the only one.'

'The only what?'

'You ain't the only toff that comes down 'ere.'

By the time they were back at Whitechapel Road, Dolly
knew that she had created a problem for herself. In her eager-
ness to get the girl away from that awful house and from her
father, she had made it seem that the Association would be
able to place her immediately, but this was not the case. An
employer had to be found, an interview must take place.
While this procedure went on the girl to be placed was
supposed to be living at home, for the Association had no
accommodation for her. It was quite likely that a prospective
employer would reject Lizzie because of her appearance or
her language.

In the street Lizzie again took her hand without speaking.

Back at the office Mr Modkin was talking to another visitor

like herself. Dolly took the agreement to Mary Tracy, who put it in a file labelled 'Elizabeth Comstock'. Then she looked at the register, and said that just at the moment there was nobody who wanted a girl as young as Lizzie, without experience.

'I expect there will be something soon, perhaps in the next week. Mrs Ross will let you know as soon as there is a post for which you might be suitable.'

'What's that mean?' the girl asked Dolly. 'Ain't there no jobs like you said?'

There had been few occasions in her life when Dolly had acted on impulse, and indeed she disapproved of doing so. It was with a feeling of astonishment that she heard herself saying, 'I'll take her. We need a young housemaid.'

Mary's face rarely showed emotion, but now she looked as if she thought Dolly was insane.

'Are you sure?'

'Quite sure.' She looked down at the little dark girl beside her. 'You'd like to come with me, wouldn't you, Lizzie?'

There was no change of expression on the small pinched face. 'All right,' she said, although it sounded like 'Orright.'

On the way back to Dereham Gardens Dolly considered what she had done. For reasons of economy they kept only a cook, a housemaid and a scullery maid. As Flora the house-maid had frequently said, she had far more than enough to do. There should be a parlourmaid to wait at table, dust and polish, do all the things for which Flora could not find time, but one look at Lizzie made it plain that she would not be able to fill such a role. Perhaps she could be called an under-housemaid and set to scrub steps, polish brass, clean boots and shoes, carry up coals and light fires. At present Jemima the scullery maid did those things. Dolly was aware that they were not well done, but would Lizzie do them any better? Looking at the little creature beside her, she was aware that she had landed herself with a problem. What would Bernard say?

What Bernard said, in a tone of utmost good humour, was, 'Why, Dolly, I didn't know you had it in you to do something like that. You make her sound like one of those persecuted creatures in a Dickens novel. Let's have her up and see what mortal shape she takes.'

Flora had been disapproving of Lizzie from the moment she saw her. 'I am sorry to tell you, madam, that the young person is not clean,' she had observed when Lizzie had been taken up to the attic room she was to share with Jemima. Now Flora brought in the girl, still wearing the blue and white dress because they had no uniform to fit her, and left the room with an audible sniff.

'Lizzie, this is Mr Ross.' Lizzie said nothing, looked down at the carpet. 'Lizzie, you must look at me, and answer when I speak to you.'

Lizzie looked up and said, 'Yus.'

'And you must say "madam" when you speak to me, and "sir" when you speak to Mr Ross.' The girl looked so bewildered that Dolly felt a twitch, as though some wire had been pulled within her body. 'Say "yes, madam".'

'Yes, madam.'

'We shall get you a uniform tomorrow, and you will start work then. Has Flora told you your duties?'

'Yes, madam.'

Oh dear, Dolly thought, it's hopeless, how ever could I have supposed it would work in a small household like ours. She would have been better off in a place with twenty or thirty servants.

Bernard went over and lifted her chin. He said, in a Cockney accent Dolly had never heard him use, 'Cheer up, my little cock sparrer, you ain't dead yet.'

The girl looked at him, at first uncertainly, then with something that might have been called a smile.

'That's it,' Bernard said in his usual voice. 'I like to see smiling faces. Now, Lizzie, things must seem strange here, they always do when you move to a different place and see new people. I know, because I've done it myself. But if you just try to think "This is my new life, the old one's finished", you'll feel more cheerful. This is better than where you came from, or so Mrs Ross tells me. And if you need help, just come to Mrs Ross. Do you understand?'

'Yes.'

'Yes, sir.'

'Yes, sir.' She did not take her gaze off Bernard.

'Remember that Mrs Ross will be watching, looking after you, and she will know if you do your work properly.'

Lizzie nodded. Dolly said that she could go and Lizzie left the room, taking a last fascinated glance at Bernard over her shoulder.

He shook his head laughing, after she had gone. 'Extraordinary little creature. The Lord forgive me for talking to her like a temperance lecturer. But you've chosen well, she'll settle down.'

'You did seem to know how to talk to her.' She could not help letting a tinge of disapproval enter her voice, rather as though she felt that to be wrong.

'Why, I saw dozens or hundreds like her when I first came to England. Some sweat out their lives and ruin their eyesight working as seamstresses, some go on the streets. If they're lucky they find a household like this one.'

'You don't think I've been foolish? I said we'd pay her thirty pounds a year, and she won't be worth that until she's trained.'

71

'I don't suppose that will break us. Don't worry about it.'

He asked what else she had been doing that day and she told him, but sensed that he was not paying full attention to her words. He stood by the mantelpiece, putting to his eye a little kaleidoscope that, as she knew, showed a snow scene which was transformed when you shook it into a summer day with the sun shining. At length she asked him to put it down, and he did so.

'Your sister paid a call today, an hour before you returned, together with that young art student she knows.'

'Charlie Bangs.'

'Yes, that was his name. She told a curious story about meeting some Irishmen at what she said was a club for Anarchists. I'm not sure that I approve of the places she goes to, or the company she keeps.'

'Bernard, you are being ridiculous. You sound like my father.'

'I am delighted to hear it, I have the greatest respect for him. I am not sure that your sister has enough artistic talent to justify her running around in Anarchist clubs.' She opened her mouth to protest, but before she could speak he went on. 'These were Irish Americans, and they said they would like to meet me. They gave her the address where they are staying.'

She stared. 'Do you know them?'

'I know of them. They belong to the most extreme of the Irish groups in the States. I sometimes think there is a kind of law by which political views become more extreme as those expressing them are further removed from the scene of action. Not that these men are reluctant to act. Two of them, Devas and O'Brien, were tried not long ago on a murder charge. The victim was what they would have called a traitor, a man they suspected of passing on information to a British agent. We

72

have agents reporting on what the exiles are doing in America
and France. Chicago and Paris are the two chief centres for
them as I'm sure you know.'

She did not know, but did not admit it. 'What happened at
the trial?'

'They were acquitted. Witnesses went back on their stories.
It has happened before.'

'And they were guilty?'

'I should think there's no doubt of it. The question is
whether I should see them, and what it is they want.'

She was indignant. 'You cannot think of meeting them,
Bernard, from what you say they are the lowest kind of
ruffians. I think it disgraceful that they should be admitted into
this country.'

'They have committed no crime according to the law, there
is no reason to exclude them. The question is, what do they
want? I think I should have them round here and find out. It
was you who were saying only a few days ago that I should be
talking to all sorts and conditions of Irishmen. I don't suppose
you'd care to ask them to dinner?'

'You cannot be serious.'

'One of your charms, my love, is that you mistake my levity
for seriousness, and treat my serious suggestions as jokes. But
you are quite right, a whole evening of their company would
be too much, though Devas is said to be an amusing fellow.
They were involved in a fight when Nelly saw them, something which delighted her. But I'll have them round for an
hour one afternoon, and you need not set eyes on them. I'll
make sure they don't leave an infernal machine in the hall.'

'It isn't a matter for joking. If you insist that they should
come to the house I certainly want to be here.'

He burst out laughing, and took her in his arms. 'Dolly, I

73

love you. What rational woman ever said or did more irrational things?'

As he held her close and she looked at his face, she thought him the most beautiful man she had ever seen. Now he took her hands, and said, 'Remember, Dolly, that for me as for Lizzie the past is as though it had never been. It no longer exists. Our lives belong to the present, our hopes lie in the future.'

He embraced her again. Even while she was in his arms and thinking that those were splendid phrases about past, present and future, another part of her was reflecting that they were a true politician's phrases, in the sense that she was not sure what they meant, or whether they had any meaning at all.

5 *A Good Day for the Governor*

Joseph Blader reached his office punctually at nine o'clock each morning. His secretary had already been there for half an hour, and his correspondence was sorted into matters needing immediate attention, those that could be dealt with at leisure, and matters of little importance. He read the first pile with care, called in one of his two shorthand writers and dictated letters, moving on then to the second pile. Many of these were speculative propositions that required considerable thought. Upon his desk was a text from the great Napoleon, which he had had specially printed: *If I appear to be ever ready and equal to an occasion, it is because everything is turned over in my mind again and again before I have decided on a course of action.* He often pointed out the text to those who worked for him.

Blader was a company promoter. He employed several clerks, and a lawyer named Comber who was kept permanently occupied in making sure that the articles of incorporation drawn up for each company were legally watertight. A number of young men like Roderick were also often to be seen about the office. They all called him the governor, and although they were not actually employed by him he was always ready to listen to their ideas for new business. If the business was somehow profitable, or if they introduced members of the nobility prepared to see their names on a prospectus for a Blader company, they were handsomely rewarded. Few of them got away without being given a short lecture on reciprocal aid. 'You help me, I'll help you,' the governor would say as he pushed an envelope containing their commission across the desk to them, so that they should not be offended by the sight of money. 'As my old dad used to say, it's not helping yourself, it's helping other people makes the wheels go round.' Had his father, who had been a railway porter, said such things? At all events, the governor said them, and when he talked the people who worked with him listened.

Was Joseph Blader a financial genius, or was he a crook? It was a question often debated in City chop houses, without any decisive answer being reached. Perhaps Blader did not know the answer himself, any more than he could have said whether at any given moment he was solvent. The interlocking structure of his companies was so confusing, and the mergers between them so frequent, that as Birmingham and District Tramways, Wolverhampton and West Bromwich Steam Engines and Coventry Public Transport were all merged into the Midlands Steam Transport Company, and that in its turn became part of the Great Northern and Midlands Wheeled Vehicle Company, it was hard to say whether the original shareholders were better off or not. This was especially difficult to discover when the shifts of shares were not from one tramway company to another, but from a transport company to a South American tin mine, to an asphalt company in Trinidad or to an American brewery. The shareholder might make a personal appeal to Blader, who had launched the company, asking for his money back and it was the governor's claim that those who asked had never been refused, but the new share offer would seem so evidently a bargain that shareholders demanding the return of their investment were rare. 'A man who puts down a pound as his stake, and picks up that same pound a couple of years later, will never make a million,' as Blader said.

The process by which a tramway company in the Midlands

was converted (so to speak) into a Bolivian tin mine was known as reconstruction. Sometimes the tramway company went into voluntary liquidation, but the shareholders were given the chance to take shares in Bolivian tins on very favourable terms; sometimes the new company absorbed the tramway and made a further stock issue to obtain new capital for development. All this was done in proper form, at directors' meetings held in the governor's Board Room with its impressively heavy mahogany table and chairs. There Sir Charles This and Lord That would sit and listen to the latest scheme of reconstruction, which was read out to them at speed by Mr Comber the lawyer. Then the governor would come in, tell them that the future of the reconstructed company was bright, and would read out reports from an engineer in Bolivia. The directors would approve, toast the success of the reconstruction in champagne, pocket their cheques for attending, and go home.

It was in relation to such work that Bernard Ross had been immensely useful. His head for figures was remarkable. He could run through a set of accounts and tell you in five minutes whether a company looked solvent, or lay his finger on whatever seemed doubtful in the statement of their assets. He could juggle with the complicated share details of a reconstruction involving not just two but several companies so that Blader himself could hardly follow all the details of the structure that was being devised, in which one company supported another so that the whole pyramid stood firm. Ross had begun by working on commission like the other young men, but he was now paid a salary, and frequently took the governor's place at board meetings, dazzling Sir Charles This and Lord That by his display of figures. Blader himself was slightly awed.

'There's no flies on you, my lad, and that's a fact,' he said after a board meeting at which Bernard had estimated the profits to be made through a reconstruction in so much detail and at such speed as to be almost incomprehensible. 'I swear I don't know where you get it from, when your father was a farmer.'

'I took a class in commerce at night school.'

'You're a wonder. I've said it before and I'll say it again, you're wasting your time in the House of Commons. I don't understand why you don't see it, just now especially.'

He was referring to the fact that the House of Lords had very decisively thrown out the Home Rule Bill, so that it was back with the Commons, and the whole procedure must be gone through again. So far Mr Gladstone had refused to give up, but there was a general feeling even in his own party that the old man must eventually do so, and that Irish Home Rule was a lost cause, at least in this Parliament.

'The Bill's not dead yet,' Bernard said. 'And even if it were, there are other issues that interest me which are very much alive and kicking.'

'I tell you what I'd do if you came with me, I'd make you a junior partner. My dad used to say never take a partner, you double your mistakes and take twice the time making up your mind whether to pass the salt, but there are exceptions. What d'you say?'

'It's good of you. But I want to stay in Parliament.'

'I can see the sense of that up to a point. To be able to put M.P. after your name, that's an asset in business.'

'No, I'm serious about it. I hope to get a Government post. I look forward to a long Parliamentary career. And there's another point. At present I'm happy to present the details about companies as you give them to me. If I were a partner, even a junior partner, I might want to ask questions.'

'You could ask all the questions you liked,' Blader said heartily. 'But I'll leave it for the time being. The country's gain is the City's loss, that's all I can say. You know I'll always be straight with you, and if you change your mind, let me know.'

Bernard Ross gave his slightly enigmatic smile, and said he was much honoured. As Blader said to his wife Bella, he sometimes wished he had Bernard for a son-in-law instead of that thick-headed Roderick. He did not, however, wish it always, for there were occasions when Bernard's acuteness made him a little uncomfortable, almost as though he were the novice and Bernard the financial wizard, instead of the other way round. He was glad that Bernard Ross was not present that morning, when he saw Gabriel Harris.

Gabriel had been introduced by Roderick. The two had been contemporaries at school. 'He was the most awful swot when he was a kid, always mucking about with chemicals and stuff,' Roderick said. 'Don't know what happened to him after that, then bumped into him one day and he's a partner now in some potty little firm that makes a special kind of lawn mower. As far as I can tell it hasn't caught on, but there's another thing he invented which sounds dashed interesting. I think you should have a look at it, governor.'

He had seen Harris, and had looked at the invention. It lay on his desk now, a small black cylinder. A fountain pen.

Of course Blader had seen fountain pens before, they had developed a lot in the last few years from the "reservoir pen" as they used to be called, and were now really popular, in defiance of the old slogan used in advertising:

They come as a boon and a blessing to men,
The Pickwick, the Owl, and the Waverley pen.

The Pickwick, the Owl and the Waverley were all dip pens, and there were people who said that just as the metal pen nib

79

had replaced the quill, so the Swan, Parker and other fountain pens would replace the pen that had constantly to be dipped into an ink bottle. Most fountain pens worked by a little lever which pressed on a rubber tube, and enabled you to fill the tube with sufficient ink to last for an hour or two of writing use. Harris's fountain pen, however, was different. According to him it was everlasting, or at least would not run dry for a year.

Harris was not an impressive figure. Although no more than Roderick's age, he was almost bald. His jacket sleeves were frayed, his collar not quite clean, and the bow tie beneath the collar was askew. His eyes shone brilliantly behind thick pebbled glasses, and he had a high-pitched laugh which showed yellow horse-like teeth.

'Look here,' he had said at their first interview. He unscrewed the top of the pen to reveal a blank space where the rubber filling device was normally seen. He took a small box from his pocket, opened it to reveal some thin metal tubes, took out one of them, fixed it in a slot within the pen, screwed on the top, and offered it to Blader. 'Try it.'

Blader tried it. The pen certainly wrote, with what appeared to be ink.

'Try to smudge what you've written. Go on, try.'

Blader ran his finger over the writing of his own name, but the ink did not smudge. Harris gave his high-pitched laugh. 'Write something else, try to smudge it, try to rub it out. Can't be done.'

'What is this?'

'It's the Harris Fountain Pen. Guaranteed to last for one year without running dry. Patent taken out to prevent possible imitations.'

'I meant, what's in that metal tube, what makes it write?'

80

'Ah *hah,* wouldn't you like to know? That's the Harris secret process.'

'There's no filling device.'

'No need for it.'

Blader looked at the pen dubiously. 'You say it will work for a year without refilling?'

'A year *at least.* May work as long as eighteen months. When it runs dry, just slot in another tube.'

Never show interest when you feel it. This precept, which might have come from his old dad, was well-known to Blader. He pushed the pen back across the desk and said harshly, 'What do you expect me to do about it?'

The bulging eyes glared at him from behind the pebbled lenses. 'It can't fail. All it needs is backing, to form a company, make the pen, advertise it. The Harris Wonder Pen, Outlasts All Others.'

'I should need to try the pen for a longer period, to see if it meets your claims.'

'By all means. As long as you like.'

'And to know the process of manufacture, the cost, the ingredients.'

'The cost, very low, less than a penny for each tube. The process and the ingredients, well, I may look green but I'm not a cabbage. You get them after we've signed an agreement.'

That had been three weeks ago. Blader had used the pen during that time, and found that it worked perfectly. He had allowed friends to use it, without mentioning its long-lasting properties, merely saying that it was a new kind of fountain pen, and they had agreed that it wrote very smoothly. He had pressed Harris into giving him the formula for the metal tubes, so that the cost of production could be worked out accurately. The formula meant nothing to him, but he had been told that

81

it consisted of several chemicals blended together, with a thickening and colouring agent of a harmless kind. The production cost would be no greater than Harris had said. There seemed no reason why the Everlasting Pen Company would need to be reconstructed. He had Comber draw up an agreement, and the meeting that morning was for the purpose of signing it.

That should have been a formality, but it was not. Harris arrived a quarter of an hour late with a companion named Polk, whom he introduced as his solicitor. Harris said with his laugh, 'I'm a fool with papers, don't know what I'm looking at, Jimmy's an old friend.'

Blader said nothing, but indicated disapproval by a downward turn of the mouth, a look of doubt on his usually cheerful plump face. He made a gesture indicating that Comber should pass over the agreement. Polk, a long-nosed lantern-jawed man, took a pencil from his pocket and began to go through the draft line by line, making a sound like a humming top as he did so. Harris folded his arms and sat smiling idiotically, occasionally showing his teeth. Blader felt that it was beneath his dignity to stay in the room, told Comber to let him know when Mr Harris was ready to sign, and returned to his own office.

It was nearly half-an-hour before he was called back. Comber, whose face was red and round where Polk's was long and yellow, said, 'They're not prepared to sign, governor.'

Polk tapped the papers in front of him. His voice was dry and rusty, as though his throat needed oiling. 'This agreement gives my client only five per cent of the profit from his own invention.'

'*After* Mr Blader has made a down payment of five hundred pounds to Mr Harris,' Comber said. 'An advance that is not likely to be earned for some time, perhaps never. Five hundred pounds is not to be sneezed at.' Polk raised his upper lip in what was certainly not a preliminary to a sneeze, but might have been called a sneer. 'Might I remind you also that Mr Blader will have the cost of manufacturing the pen, and will have to spend large sums in advertising and selling it. In other words, Mr Blader takes all the risks.'

'No doubt all such costs will be deducted before assessing the profits.' There could be no doubt that Polk was sneering now.

'Suppose there are no profits? Your client is still five hundred pounds to the good.'

Polk shook his head. 'My understanding is that such a possibility does not arise. There will be such a demand for the pen that it cannot fail.'

'The merest guesswork,' Comber said, his face very red.

Blader intervened. 'Has Mr Polk made a suggestion?'

Comber said, as though he could hardly believe it, 'He has suggested sixty per cent of all profits to Mr Harris, forty per cent to you.'

Blader looked hard at the two lawyers, then turned to leave the room. Harris, who had been sitting with his fixed grin, said in alarm, 'Where are you going?'

'There is no point in further discussion. You can take your pen somewhere else, Mr Harris.'

'But you've tested the pen. You know it works.'

'The pen appears to work, yes. That is only the beginning. This is something completely new, nobody knows what problems we may meet when we come to produce it.'

'I've told you already, it will be very cheap to produce.'

Blader rarely raised his voice, but when he did the effect had cowed more than one meeting of recalcitrant stockholders.

83

'*You've* told me, yes, but why should I accept that? Mr Harris, I am prepared to put *my* resources and *my* time into marketing *your* invention. You take no risk of any sort, and you ask for more than half the profits. Very well, you can take your lawyer with you, and see if you can do better elsewhere. I have other things to occupy me, I can tell you. Don't come back to me when you've failed to get backing elsewhere, that's all I ask. I don't like my time wasted.'

Harris took off the thick glasses, revealing blue bewildered eyes. Polk said creakingly, 'That is unreasonable, Mr Blader. We are here to negotiate.'

'With the kind of figures you've mentioned, negotiation is impossible. Good day and good luck, gentlemen.'

Polk retained his sneer, but Harris sounded on the verge of tears as he said that he only wanted what was reasonable.

'Nobody can say I'm unreasonable. Mr Comber, is five per cent unreasonable?'

'In view of what you'll have to lay out I'd call it generous, governor.'

'I couldn't advise Mr Harris to accept less than fifty per cent,' Polk said.

Blader left them to it. Half an hour later Comber came in, and told him that Harris had settled for fifteen per cent of the profits after all costs were met. The solicitor was full of admiration. 'I never thought we'd get them down to less than thirty, governor. It was your idea of the five hundred down that did it. He didn't want to lose that.'

Blader nodded, and lighted a Corona. 'That and his stupid solicitor friend. I'd lay a bet he was the one who pitched it at sixty per cent, much too high. Make a silly demand like that and you're in no position to bargain when it's turned down, you have to drop too much. We'll get production in hand as soon as may be. That little article's a gold mine, Comber, take it from me.'

The day that had begun so well continued still better. In the afternoon Blader had an appointment with an American named Duncan J. Hatherley. It was not unusual for American business men in London to approach him, generally with a view to getting backing for companies they owned in the United States, companies brewing local beers or starting up a new railroad. One or two of these gentlemen had proved to be uncommonly sharp practitioners, like the man who had tried to get him to handle breweries in states with very restrictive liquor laws, so that the outfit concerned was little more than a name on a piece of paper. After being bitten twice, Blader had been careful to check on the existence and prospects of any American company offered him.

Duncan J. Hatherley, however, was on quite another tack. He was a tall, handsome man, perhaps in his late thirties. His top hat had a splendid sheen, his silk cravat was elegant, his trousers beautifully pressed, and his manner was as perfect as his dress. Or so it seemed to Blader, who disliked the breezy briskness of some American business men, perhaps because it slightly resembled his own.

'I'm much obliged to you for sparing time to see me,' Hatherley said. 'You'll like to see some credentials.' The letters he presented included one from J. Pierpont Morgan and another from the president of the Chase National Bank, saying that they had known Mr Hatherley for several years, and had found him entirely straightforward in his business dealings. Blader returned them, offered the American a cigar, and asked how he could be of help.

Hatherley leaned back in his chair and smiled. 'You can advise me about making some English investments, Mr Blader.

85

You look a little surprised, and I guess you mostly get requests the other way round, for you to back an American company. But I'll tell you how it is with me. I've been lucky in the States, they sometimes call me Lucky Hatherley and say I've got the Midas touch. I only have to show interest in a company over there and the shares go up. That's no use to me as a man of business, so I've come across the water to see if Lucky Hatherley can stay lucky over here.'

'You mean you'd like to invest in a company I'm concerned with? I take that as a compliment, a very real compliment. Of course I'd want you first of all to be assured about the company's prospects. I shouldn't expect you to take my word for it.'

The American waved his cigar. 'A run through the balance sheet will be enough. You'd like to know the form of payment, I don't doubt. It will depend on the size of the investment, but mostly it will be payment by bearer bills or something similar. You won't be at risk.'

Blader's mind had been at work ever since he learned Hatherley's intention. The American must be shrewder than he appeared, or he could never have made money in the States. It wouldn't do to land him with shares in a company due for reconstruction, or one likely to be merged with another in a couple of months. This was not the time for anything risky. He recommended two companies, a steamship line, and a company recently formed to exploit the gold mines of Siberia, saying frankly that the first was a sound proposition and that the second was exciting but chancy, depending as it did on reports from a mining engineer which suggested that Siberia might be the fifth gold-producing country in the world. The first was a sure thing, the second a speculation. Hatherley thanked him and took away the documents, which included the report of Bogdanovitch, the Russian mining engineer. Later in the afternoon the papers were returned, with a note saying: *A man who never risked a dollar never made a dollar. Siberian gold for me!* He went on to observe that he was studying the market closely, and hoped that this would be the first of many pleasant dealings. With the letter, which came from the Savoy Hotel, was enclosed a bill at three months made payable to bearer. The bill was saleable in the market, and so was as good as cash.

Blader went home that night feeling very pleased with himself.

6   *Sunday Lunch at Highgate*

On the Sunday after Blader had had his good day in the City, the Detling family visited the Blader home at Highgate for Sunday luncheon. It was rarely that the families saw each other socially, and this particular gathering had come about only because Matilda had suddenly decided that they should all spend Christmas at Chadderley House, which was the name of the Detlings' place in Kent. The decision was perhaps prompted chiefly by the disastrous failure of a musical occasion she had given especially to launch the work of a young pianist recommended to her as a prodigy. The pianist had attempted Chopin's *Fantaisie Impromptu*, and was manifestly not up to it. Perhaps some Mendelssohn would have been better, or perhaps he was just incompetent, but in any case the result had been painful. Friends were caustic, which was unpleasant, or sympathetic, which was unbearable.

The experience had prompted in Matilda a longing for country life which she felt only when things went badly in town. At such times she spoke of the discontent she had always felt with bricks and mortar, and of the natural human longing for trees and greenness and peace. It would be wonderful, she said, to spend a real country English Christmas at Chadderley. They would be altogether removed from the artificiality of urban life, there would be blazing log fires and they would play the old games of Christmas, snapdragon and hunt the slipper and charades. And of course it must be a family Christmas, for she had no intention of being landed down at Chadderley House with only her husband for company. It was to resolve the problems of Christmas, for problems they turned out to be, that they all met at Crossways, which was the name of the Blader residence.

Crossways was a modern villa, which contained such refinements as electric lighting and running hot water. There was a telephone installed, so that Blader could be in touch with his City office at any time, and a heated swimming pool in which he did twenty lengths each morning. There was too much of everything at Crossways. It was very well to have enough servants, but here there were so many that they seemed positively to crowd round the guests, taking away hats and coats, opening doors, dusting chairs, offering little biscuits, and then later on appearing in extraordinary multiplicity in the dining room, so that one set of maidservants handed round the soup, another took the plates away, and a third brought in the fish course, while a fourth (although perhaps it was really the first again) was responsible for the roast beef, with its vegetables and sauces, the ham and the tongue. The meat plates had some sort of crest on them which was certainly not that of the railway porter's family, and the pudding plates that succeeded them were rimmed thickly with gold. Sir Arthur provided an accompaniment of muttering discontent at the lavishness of the meal, particularly when he was offered three kinds of mustard.

'Eh?' he said. 'What are those?'

The little girl serving the mustards remained mute. Bella Blader, a broad-faced broad-bottomed woman who retained traces of her native Yorkshire accent, said 'English, French or German mustard, Sir Arthur. It's nice to have a bit of variety sometimes, don't you think?'

'English is good enough for me.'

'Isn't it funny? Joe has a taste for the German.' His wife was the only person who called Blader Joe.

Sir Arthur grunted. He was not pleased to be eating away from home on Sunday, and resented being brought all the way out to Highgate to discuss Matilda's nonsensical idea. It was all odious to him, the lavishness of the food, the butler carving the beef, the ostentatious display of wealth. He pushed the food about on his plate, murmuring rebellion against it. Blader held up his glass, so that the wine shone in the electric lamps of the chandelier.

'A nice glass of burgundy. I made sure it was decanted three hours before it was served, which is the time they say should be allowed. Anything more and some of the freshness has gone, leave it later and the wine's got no time to breathe. That's what they call it, you know, breathe. What do you say, Roderick, Bernard?'

'Perfect,' Roderick said. 'Couldn't be better.'

'Nobody born in America can presume to offer an opinion on wine,' Bernard replied. 'We merely drink it.'

That was said with what Dolly thought of as his politician's smoothness. She knew that a lady, like an American, was not expected to comment on wine, but saw no reason why this should stop her. 'It has a pleasant flavour, but seems to me rather strong for luncheon,' she said. Nelly, who was there with Charlie Bangs, gave a quickly suppressed giggle.

'What do you say, Sir Arthur?'

Sir Arthur glared in his host's direction. 'Never heard an Englishman talk about wine before.'

Blader's good humour, with thoughts of the Everlasting Pen and that splendid speculative American strong in his mind, was such that he took no offence.

The discussion about Christmas came afterwards, in the drawing room. This was filled with what was said to be Louis Quinze furniture, which Bella had been told was just the thing for a fashionable drawing room. Whether or not this was so, the chairs and sofas were not very comfortable, and Sir Arthur went off to smoke a pipe in Blader's study.

Matilda was in a businesslike mood. She had equipped herself with a large writing pad on which to make notes. 'I should like it to be a real Christmas family party. I hope there's no doubt about you and Mr Blader.'

'You must ask my lord and master.'

Blader caressed his chin. Gertrude said, 'You know you always say Christmas is a waste of time, papa, that it interferes with the natural course of business.' She spoke as always in a tone of defiance, as though she were resisting an attempt to force her to do something against her will. 'It is a long journey down to Kent, and we have to think of little Billy.'

'There are plenty of trains from London,' Dolly said with some tartness. 'And the journey is not much more than two hours. I don't see why Billy should come to any harm in a railway coach. What do you say, Roderick?'

'Makes no odds as far as I'm concerned,' her brother said cheerfully. He appeared not to see his wife's meaningful glance. 'Always enjoyed Christmas down at Chadderley. Rattling good idea, I'd say.'

'Roderick, you know we have arranged to spend Christmas Day here with papa and mamma.'

'Oh yes, of course, I mean to say, it all depends on the governor. If you're staying in town why then, as Gertrude says, we'll come over.'

Dolly thought, not for the first time, that her brother was a feeble fool, and that she was glad to have married a man who might be almost too invariably polite, but would not be wound round any woman's little finger. However, Blader now spoke weightily, rather as though he were pronouncing a decision on the life and death, or the need for reconstruction, of a company.

'Quite true that I may have matters of importance to decide over the Christmas holiday. But it's a time for jollification, and I think we ought to be jolly. If, Matilda my dear, you can put up with a business man who might – mind you, I only say might – have to be called away on something of urgent importance while the crackers are being pulled, then we should be honoured to accept.'

'Especially since we haven't had the pleasure of visiting Chadderley House before,' Bella added.

Matilda gave her vague smile, and said she hoped that meant Roderick and Gertrude would join the party. Gertrude reluctantly admitted that it would. Matilda turned to her daughters.

'I don't know,' Nelly said. 'They work us awfully hard at the Slade.'

'That isn't what I've heard,' her brother said. 'I've heard it's nothing but drinking filthy stuff like absinthe, and parties in disgusting studios, everything higgledy-piggledy on filthy old tables, not even a proper bedroom. Bally degrading, I call it.'

'Really, Roderick, you are ridiculous.'

'Oh, am I? Well, I still say it's bally degrading,' he repeated, and went to join his father in the study. Nelly resumed.

'What I said is true. The teachers get awfully peppery if you don't turn up, isn't that true, Charlie?' Charlie Bangs, who had been invited to lunch as Nelly's young man, nodded. 'But I suppose a few days wouldn't matter. For either of us.'

The last words were not lost upon her mother. 'Of course I should like Christmas to be a real cornucopia of family and friends. I hope very much that you will join us, Mr Baines.'

'Mamma, Charlie's name is not Baines, it is Bangs. And I think these conventions are ridiculous. You should call him Charlie.'

93

Charlie had coloured slightly. 'I should very much like to come down to Kent. My home is in Ireland, and by the time I get there I should have to come back, if you'll pardon the Irishism. I was going to spend Christmas in my lodgings.'

Matilda beamed at him, and made notes. 'Dolly, I hope you and Bernard are free.'

'Of course we shall come down, mamma, but not for long. I have my duties in Whitechapel, and Roderick must go back.'

'I thought you M.P.s had an easy time of it,' Charlie said, laughing.

'Not this year. We have only recently finished the longest session in history, from January to September, and now we are to convene again at the beginning of next month. We are still battling on Home Rule, and Mr Gladstone is threatening to keep us there very nearly until Christmas. But if you'll blame him for any early departure we make, Christmas in the country would be delightful.'

Matilda's country vision had become so strong that she hardly listened. 'And babbled of green fields,' she said. 'I always think that is one of the Bard's most beautiful lines. The green fields, the church bells chiming the hour, how lovely they are. Here in London the bells have a leaden ring.'

'Mamma, it was Falstaff who babbled about green fields when he was dying, and the fields will be full of mud in this weather. But there is something you haven't mentioned. Have you told Bateman?'

'Whoever said it, the line is beautiful.' Matilda reluctantly brought back her thoughts to the present. 'Not yet.'

'Then the house will never be ready. You know what he's like.'

'I take it Bateman is some kind of family retainer,' Blader said. Nelly giggled.

94

'Yes, you could call him that.'

'Does it matter what he's like? If he is told to get the house ready, surely he has ample time to do it.'

'You don't know Bateman. He's, oh, *ages* old, been at Chadderley before I was born, when grandfather was alive. And he really runs the place, nothing can be done unless Bateman says so.'

Blader stuck out his chin. 'That seems ridiculous. He is a servant, and should do what he is told.'

The phrase permeated to Matilda, who had been making notes on her pad. 'I don't think you quite understand, Joseph. We regard Bateman as one of the family.'

Had she intended a rebuke? Dolly wondered. One could never be sure how much of Matilda's sweetness and vagueness was real, how much assumed. She thought also about Bateman, with exasperation rather than affection. In her childhood he had been a tyrant, an old man who was always appearing suddenly and telling them not to do things. Her feeling for efficiency was outraged by the fact that for more than half the year Bateman had nothing to do but look after the servants wastefully kept in occupation during the long periods when nobody from the family was down at Chadderley. This had never stopped him from complaining of overwork when given notice of a visit.

'I shall send a telegram,' Matilda said. She wrote down Telegram, and underlined it. 'Today. Now perhaps we should see when everybody will be coming.'

Roderick found his father in the study, half asleep, with the Sunday newspapers on his lap.

'Father, it's settled that we're going down to Chadderley for Christmas. The Bladers are coming – the governor says he can take a few days away from business, although he may have to come up to town if he's needed urgently. And of course Gertrude and I will be coming.' Sir Arthur grunted. 'Only one thing worries me, Bateman. If I know him he won't have the place half ready, and it's not the thing when we've got the governor coming down, makes a bad impression. Can't you put him in a cottage, get somebody younger?'

Sir Arthur grunted again, then suddenly snapped to attention. 'What's that you said? Bateman's been there I don't know how long. Before you were born.'

'My point exactly. He's not up to the mark now, can't expect him to be.'

'Oh indeed. And I'm to get rid of him to please Joseph Blader, is that what you're saying?'

'Not only for that reason, of course. I was giving an opinion, that's all.'

'And who asked for your opinion?' Father and son looked very similar as they sat opposite each other in the study, two weak men with strong faces. 'Bateman has been a loyal servant of the family, and I shall be glad if you will remember it. When I am gone you may do as you like, but while I am still here I decide about such matters.'

Too late Roderick saw that he had erred in mentioning Bateman as an introduction to the matter that really concerned him. He tried to shift responsibility for what he had been saying. 'I feel as strongly about Bateman as you do, but he is getting on. I know Dolly feels he should be put out to grass.'

'What does she know about it, married to a tuppenny-ha'penny politician, and forever mixing with those disreputable people down in Whitechapel? One daughter spending her time with Jews and Lascars, the other dirtying herself among a lot of paint brushes. If my father could have seen it he'd have turned in his grave. But that's the way things are nowadays.'

He showed signs of composing himself for sleep. Roderick said desperately, 'I did want to ask your advice. Advice and help.' There was no comment. 'This is a bally difficult time, as I expect you know. Having a family turns out to be bally expensive.'

'One son. A year old.' Little blue eyes looked at him balefully.

'Yes, of course, one as you say. Another on the way, as a matter of fact. Gertrude has just had it confirmed by the doctor.'

'My congratulations. Very good news. Hardly unexpected, however.'

'Yes, of course that's true. It's good news as you say, but it leaves me deuced short of the ready. I wondered if you might see your way to a small loan. I'd give you a note for it, naturally. I don't suppose I shall need it more than six months.'

'You have been gambling again.' His son did not deny it. 'What is the sum of money?'

'It's really two thou, but I can manage with fifteen hundred.'

Two thousand pounds.' Sir Arthur sat bolt upright. He had lent, or given, his son money before to pay his debts, but the sum involved had never been more than five hundred.

'I've not asked you for anything for some time. These things mount up.'

'Are you out of your mind, Roderick? Do you think you can gamble away a fortune, and then come to me for the money? I can tell you that you've come to the wrong place. I never was a rich man, I've made provision for one of your sisters, and by the time I've done the same for Nelly I shouldn't be surprised if I end up a pauper. If you want your debts covered, you'd better go to *the governor* as you call him. Perhaps he will give you a parcel of shares in one of his fifty companies, and you can pass them on to your creditors. That's what life has come to, bits of paper taking the place of sovereigns in your pockets. It's all one with the Government kow-towing to those Irish villains your brother-in-law loves so much. All of a piece, all of a piece.'

'Then you won't help me.'

'You must stand on your own feet, Roderick. You have a job, although as far as I can understand you are paid for sitting with your feet up on a desk. You go about among young sparks with money to burn. Do as you please, it's none of my business, but don't come to me to pay your debts.'

That was the end of the interview.

7 *Two Weeks in November*

That Sunday lunch at Highgate took place on the last Sunday in October. Several events took place in the first two weeks of November that bore upon the final tragedies.

Matilda followed up her telegram to Bateman with a letter. No doubt the telegram was hardly necessary if one considered the length of time that stretched between the end of October and Christmas, but it expressed her own feeling of urgency, her delight at the prospect of country life. The letter gave specific details about getting the rooms ready, and about the likely number of guests.

Would it be better to go down to Chadderley for a week or two, and superintend the arrangements? Perhaps, but Matilda did not want to be down there by herself. Her idea of country life was that it should be a relaxation from the intellectual and artistic strain of London. She envisaged it as a continuous house party, with lots of young people present, picnics at beauty spots, walks in sunny gardens, some shooting and fishing and then billiards in the evening, the men all rather gallant and the ladies flirting with them. It was a vision that she could hardly hope to realise at this time of year, but the family gathering at Christmas held promise. She was delighted to hear from Roderick that a friend of his from the office was at a loose end, and said that she would be most happy for Paul Patterwick to join them. She had hoped that some of Bernard's fellow Members of Parliament might be free, but Bernard smilingly told her that all his friends were too grand to accept an invitation or too humble to be given one. She waited more than a week before receiving a reply to her letter to

Chadderley, something which did not surprise her because she knew that word of the visit would come as a shock to Bateman. The letter, in Bateman's copperplate hand, was brief:

My Lady,

Your telegram and letter have arrived. I regret to inform you that Mrs Maitland has left, due to a disagreement. Also part of the cellar has been flooded. You will appreshiate my difficulties, but I shall do my best to have all in order for your arrival.

Respectfully, J. Bateman.

Mrs Maitland had been the housekeeper, and she was not the first in that position to have left because of a disagreement with Bateman about the range of her authority. The news might have been thought a little disquieting, but she did not find it so. When she had Bateman's letter she regarded the whole matter of Christmas at Chadderley as settled, and put it out of her mind. That failure with the Chopin had turned her away from music, but she went to a number of art exhibitions, in hope of finding a young painter who had not been taken up by the critics. With this in mind she had asked to see some of Charlie Bangs's work, but had been disconcerted to find that most of his paintings showed the interiors of grimy and dismal public houses, while his drawings were of street vendors and slatternly women with their children. She spoke to Nelly.

'Charlie is such a nice young man. Why does he have to depict such sordid scenes and such dirty people?'

Nelly, who in her mother's view was getting a little above herself, said that Charlie painted life, and that if Matilda wanted picture postcard art she would find plenty of it at the Royal Academy.

In fact, Nelly herself was surprised by the kind of work Charlie

100

Bangs produced. Most of the other students acted as models for each other, although none of the girls cared to pose in the nude, but Charlie persuaded cleaners and street arabs to come and sit for him, paying them no more than a copper or two. He had also made several drawings of Mrs Cable, the bewigged landlady, whom he showed almost as a Dickens character done by Cruikshank.

'That's cruel, Charlie,' she said about one of them. 'It's a caricature. What does Mrs Cable think of it?'

'She loves it. And you're wrong, you know. When she's bringing in the tea she sticks her arms out just like that, and shoves her head to one side. Most people really look like caricatures, you know. That's why the things I've done of you are no good. You look too much like a human being.'

'I'm *like* a human being, am I? That's some consolation. I know there's one thing I'm not, and that's an artist. It's no use your being polite, I'm no good. When I see the kind of work Chris Grant does, or you do, I know I'm no good. I shall leave at the end of the year.'

They were in his Warren Street studio, and he was drawing her while she talked. He took the sheet of paper off the pad, and threw it on the floor. 'Don't do that, I shan't be able to see you.'

'Would that matter?'

'You know it would. I love you.' He kissed her, as he had done before. They had gone no further than kisses.

'Shall we run away together?'

'Why should we do that?' He placed a hand on her breast, and a delicious excitement pervaded her. 'Why not get married? Eventually, I mean.'

'Dolly's married, and I suppose Bernard's all right, but she seems to have a very boring life. And Roderick was quite nice before he married that awful Gertrude, but now –' She shivered. 'They'd never do the kind of thing we do, go to public houses, have parties. I think we should elope.'

While saying this she was aware of Charlie's lips on her neck, of Charlie's fingers fumbling with the buttons of her dress. The delicious sensation seemed to overwhelm her, and she made only mild consenting protests as he led her towards the bed. On Mrs Cable's not quite clean sheets, below a drawing of Mrs Cable holding a tray containing tea and Eccles cakes, she lost her virginity.

Roderick's Christmas invitation to Paul Patterwick had been made when his friend said what a miserable holiday he would spend with his widowed father, the Judge, who talked of nothing but his old criminal cases. They were chatting in Paul's slit of a room, a room in which both of the long walls were covered with his Irish files.

'Why not come down with me to Chadderley?' Roderick brightened at the thought. 'My mother would be pleased, she likes to get as many people around as she can. We shall play charades, we're all hot stuff at those. And we could have a few hundreds up at billiards at a fiver a time.'

Paul looked up from the papers in front of him, his pale eyes gleaming. 'Here's something interesting. One of our agents in New York has sent a copy of a letter from Jack Grogan, one of the I.R.B. heads there, written to a man named McLaverty over here, telling him that six hundred stock items as required are being sent, and that he hopes the salesmen can dispose of them. Of course it's an elementary code, the stock items are guns or bombs, and the salesmen are the men who use them. The interesting thing is that, as my records show, McLaverty's the name used by a fellow called Burns, who's supposed to be still in America. We like to keep tags on people like that. I'll have to send a memorandum to Scotland Yard to see what they know about it. Have to keep everything on paper, you know where you are when things are put down on paper.'

'I don't know how you have the head for it,' Roderick said admiringly. 'I know I wouldn't. Don't need to write more than a couple of letters a week, thank the Lord. Do you keep tags, as you call it, on all the Irish who come over here?'

'Here and in Ireland, although that's not so easy. We know every move they make. Even so –' Paul did not finish the sentence, and sat looking at the papers in front of him.

'So what about Christmas? I'd be no end pleased if you came.'

Paul said that he would like it too, and they went off to the Burlingham, where they spent an hour playing roulette. Paul ended up a winner, Roderick a loser.

'You must have a system,' Paul said afterwards, with a touch of smugness. 'I told you that's the important thing.'

'I don't know why I play here, when I always lose. I sometimes think the wheel's crooked. I have more luck at the Up and Down.' The Up and Down was another gambling club. 'But even there things haven't gone right lately.'

'Is what d'ye call him, Blader, coming down at Christmas?'

'Yes, the governor will be down.'

'Perhaps you can tap him.'

'I'm not sure he'd like it, but you're right, I think I may have to. I'm seeing him tomorrow.'

In Howland Street Eustace Settleby was preparing his paintings for an exhibition. Canvases that had been piled on top of each other in a junk room were brought out, dusted, put beside more recent work. Eustace was beside himself with excitement.

'This is my chance,' he said to Laura. 'When the critics see these pictures, all the rubbish of the Academy and the Slade will be blown right out of the window. This is the new art, they'll say, Settleby is in direct line of descent from Turner.'

Laura's hard face was grooved with sceptical lines. 'The last time you had a show, eight years ago was it, you sold two pictures.'

'They weren't ready for me,' Eustace shouted. 'Genius has to wait for recognition.'

'Give me the bottle.' They were drinking gin from dirty glasses. 'It didn't seem to me that dealer, Yarborough or whatever his name was, was enthusiastic. I don't know how you do it.'

'Genius,' the painter roared. 'He didn't want to, but he recognised it.'

'I'd like to know how often we'd have gone hungry if I didn't take off my clothes so that a lot of art students can see what a woman looks like.' She gazed blearily at him. 'If it hadn't been for me, Mr Genius Settleby, you'd be living in a Rowton House or a Sally Army hostel by now.'

Settleby seized the nearest weapon to hand, a broom with which she had been making a belated attempt to sweep up the room, and began to beat her with it. His aim was wild, but one of the blows caught her across the cheek, bringing up an immediate swelling.

'That does it,' she shrieked. 'That's the finish, I'm going, you can see how you fancy life on your own, Eustace Settleby.' A couple of minutes later she had packed her few bits of clothing in a cardboard suitcase and departed. Left to himself, the painter sat down at the old deal table used for meals and for the preparation of canvases, and repeated, 'Genius.'

'You didn't tell me that Mr Devas had written to you,' Dolly said. She had seen the note when tidying up his desk, which he liked her to do rather than leaving it to Flora. The note was headed with an address in Clerkenwell, and said: *Dear Mr Ross, I am in London with two friends, recently arrived from the United States, and think a meeting might be to our mutual benefit.*

'I told you that your sister gave me their address. I wrote to ask what they wanted. That is the reply.'

'But why should he say that a meeting will be to your mutual benefit? What benefit can you possibly derive from seeing these murderers?'

'I have told you that they were acquitted, so that they should not be spoken of as murderers. As to the benefit, perhaps they may enlarge my knowledge of Irish affairs.'

'I never know when you are joking. But as I said before, if you must see them I should like to be present.'

'You understand that there may be things they want to discuss with me in private?'

She said obstinately that even so she wished to see what they were like. The upshot was that the Irishmen were asked to luncheon.

Although she would have been reluctant to acknowledge it even to herself, Dolly was disappointed by their appearance. They all wore dark clothes of an old-fashioned cut, and O'Brien and Flaherty had thick spade beards that put her in mind of the vicar at the church she had attended when she was young. Or they might perhaps have been worthy tradesmen, good reliable grocers or chemists. Devas was different, not only because his complexion was sandy and he was clean-shaven. He had a liveliness, and an air of authority, that the others lacked.

105

At luncheon he leaned across to her, and said with a twinkle in his eye, 'It is very good of you, Mrs Ross, to be extending hospitality to such notorious firebrands as ourselves. Your husband's friend Mr MacMurdo and others in Parliament would say that you were keeping doubtful company. Or has Mr Ross kept the dark secrets of our past?'

She said coldly, 'He told me you had been tried for murder.'

O'Brien, who had been eating as though his life depended on it, raised his head, looked from one to the other of them with the confused simplicity of an ox, and then bent over his plate again.

'And acquitted,' she added.

'Or we should not be here.' Devas threw back his head and laughed. 'The truth is, Mrs Ross, that we are Fenians, we fight for Irish freedom, and by freedom we mean that we are opposed to any kind of English rule. We are not among those who would accept Mr Gladstone's kind gift of an Irish Parliament, while the land and the money remain in English hands. But perhaps you don't concern yourself with such matters.'

'On the contrary, I am very interested. I think you will find that very few people in this country, or in your own, agree with that point of view.'

'We shall hope to persuade Mr Ross to support us,' Devas said, still smiling. She looked at Bernard, and saw his hands clenched tightly on his knife and fork. It had been arranged that he would talk to them in private after luncheon, but his manner had been strained ever since their arrival.

'Whatever my husband may feel about your ends, I know he cannot approve of your methods.' As soon as she had spoken she regretted the words, since it was for Bernard to say what he thought, but his expression did not change, and he might not have heard her.

The other Irishman, Flaherty, said in a growling voice, 'We do what we have to do. If they were English and traitors to their country, how would you feel then?'

Dolly was not one to refuse such a challenge. 'My belief is that we have done wrong, very wrong, in Ireland. That can be no justification for shooting men in dark alleys, or stabbing them to death as Lord Frederick Cavendish was killed in Phoenix Park. Such methods must turn all decent people against your cause.'

'Bravo, bravo.' Devas clapped his hands. 'May I say, Mrs Ross, that I have never heard Gladstonian liberalism more eloquently expounded?'

'You are making fun of me. I don't mind that, except that you should not dismiss arguments just because they are advanced by a woman.'

At that Bernard spoke. They were among the few words he had uttered spontaneously during the meal. 'I can assure you that these gentlemen would dismiss the arguments even more briskly if they were advanced by men.'

If he knew that, since he knew that, what in the world was he doing talking to them at all? Later they all trooped off to the study and she busied herself about the house, although she felt it a deprivation that she should have to do so rather than arguing with them (she supposed they would be arguing) in the study. Instead, she listened to complaints from Flora about Lizzie's use of bad language, and then saw the girl. Lizzie looked so small in her uniform, and so much like an inquisitive bird, that Dolly felt the same emotion that had touched her when the girl had taken her hand in Whitechapel.

'Lizzie, I have to speak to you again about your language. I am told you swore at Flora, and at Jemima too.'

'Beg your pardon, madam, but it wasn't really at them.'

Even in the short time she had been in the house, Lizzie's speech had noticeably changed. She no longer said 'Yus', and her Cockney 'reelly' was now an exception. She had also been quick in learning what to do and was good at her work, so that the brass was in fact better polished now than when Jemima had done it. 'Can I say what 'appened?' An occasional aspirate was still dropped.

'Happened, Lizzie, not 'appened. Very well.'

'I was bringing up this scuttle of coal, see, and a brush and dustpan 'ad been left lying about in the passage outside the kitchen, and I stumbled over them and spilled the coal about everywhere, and asked what bleeding fool had been stupid enough to leave the bleeding brush and dustpan there. I'm sorry it slipped out, madam, but you can see it was an aggravation.'

'I can see that, but if you want to stay you must control yourself. You do your work well, but Flora tells me you answer back, and that will not do.'

'I called her an old cow, 'cause she's always on at me. Down Whitechapel they don't think anything of that.'

'Well, in Kensington we do think something of it.' Dolly felt like a governess as she continued. 'Flora is in authority over you. She is in my place, and if you wish to stay you must do as she says. However much bad language you may have used in the past, you must not use it here. You do wish to stay, don't you?'

'Oh *yes,* madam. I wouldn't do it, say those things, if it was you.'

'What do you mean?'

'If it was you instead of that Flora, I wouldn't say silly old cow. Nor swear, neither.' Lizzie began to cry. To Dolly's horror she felt again the stirrings of those almost maternal feelings that had moved her before, so that she was inclined to weep herself. She resisted, however, and sent Lizzie off rebuked but happy, with the promise that if she behaved herself she might soon be made under-parlourmaid and allowed to wait at table.

Dolly then hovered around, yes, quite consciously hovered around, until she heard the study door open, and they all came out. She could read nothing on the wooden faces of Flaherty and O'Brien, but Devas thanked her for the delightful meal, and said smilingly that he hoped they could continue their interesting discussion at another time. When they had gone she said to Bernard, 'Well?'

'I think so, yes, very well.' He had recovered his usual good spirits.

'You seemed gloomy at luncheon, now you are cheerful. What happened?'

'They wanted my support for a policy of outright British departure from Ireland. They are all from the States, as I told you, and the most fervent advocates of get-the-British-out are in America. I met people like them in Chicago when I was young. They have very little understanding of feelings in this country or in Ireland, as you rightly said. In any case, they asked for my support, and I told them they could not have it.'

'I am amazed that they are allowed to go about freely here, when Devas and O'Brien shot a man.'

'I have told you, they were acquitted. They are free to come and go in this country. When O'Donovan Rossa came here, a man known to have inspired or taken part in a number of bombing incidents, he was allowed to address a public meeting in the centre of London. Of course Scotland Yard kept an eye on him, and I don't doubt they are keeping watch on our three friends.'

'And that was all they wanted? I liked Mr Devas, he was so lively and seemed to be clever.'

'He's the brains of that little collection, one of the leaders of the Brotherhood in the States. But don't imagine that he's to be trusted, any more than the others. They're all double-dyed villains, although I daresay they believe sincerely that they are Irish patriots.'

'Was there nothing more they said?'

'Nothing that I am going to tell you,' he said, and began to laugh when he saw her look of frustration.

For the governor these were exciting days. The Everlasting Pen was put into production at a warehouse in Greenwich. Part of the place was turned into a small, very primitive laboratory, where the chemicals were blended under the supervision of a young man with a science degree, who had answered an advertisement asking for a chemicals expert. The company had been registered, and the shares would shortly be issued. Harris was being given ten per cent of them, and Blader meant to retain the rest for himself at present. He was in the position of a man who, having announced twenty times the discovery of dubious gold deposits in the mine he was panning, suddenly finds himself possessed of large, quite unquestionable gold nuggets. There was no reason why the Everlasting Pen Company should not be an immense success.

Then there was Duncan J. Hatherley. The American's appetite seemed only to have been whetted by his venture into Siberian gold mines. He had not yet made any further investments, but was in touch with Blader two or three times a week, asking what he thought of this or that stock. He had invited the governor to dinner at the Savoy, and had then asked if he might call him by that colloquialism.

'I've been told you're known as "the governor" in the City, and I can pretty well understand why,' Hatherley said with a smile. 'Should I be out of line if I called you that myself, purely as a mark of respect?'

Blader laughed, and said he would be honoured. He liked the American's frank manner, which never made him feel inferior. Some of the baronets and viscounts who had accepted invitations to serve on the boards of Blader companies had made it clear that they felt themselves to be touching pitch by association with him, and did so only because of the sovereigns attached to the pitch. There could be no doubt that Hatherley was a gentleman, even though an American gentleman was not quite the same breed as his English counterpart, and to be called governor by such a man was a compliment. Then there were those introductions from Pierpont Morgan and the Chase National Bank, which were pleasant things to see, although Blader knew that they might in some way or other be less than authentic. That possibility did not concern him, because the bond, which had been cashed, was a perfect introduction in itself. He could have sent a cable across the Atlantic asking about Hatherley's reputation, but with a man who was in effect paying cash for the shares he bought, what would have been the point?

He was thus in an excellent temper when, one day in the early afternoon, Roderick paid him a visit. The young man had come on from the Oval Table, where he had been playing whist for high stakes with no better than his usual luck. He had been told by Gertrude that it would be useless to ask her father for a loan, but necessity pressed him the other way.

Blader listened to him with good humour. 'You remember what I've said about being useful to each other? I help you, you help me, and the wheels go round. You ask me to lend you money, but how will that benefit me, what can you offer in exchange? I don't see anything, to be frank, nothing at all.'

'I thought some of the introductions I've made –'

'True, my lad, very true, but if you remember you've been paid for them. However, there's the matter of your friend Harris.' He chuckled. Roderick had rarely seen the governor so genial. 'Quite a card, Harris, isn't he? That idea he brought along, the new style of fountain pen, I believe there's something in it and I'm promoting it. I doubt if he'd get anybody else in the City to take it up, mind you, it's a risky affair, but I've got a feeling about it, and I trust my feelings. I'll tell you what I'm going to do, Roddy. You can have a hundred pounds for making the introduction, or you can take a parcel of shares that'll be worth five times that in a few months or my name's not Joe Blader. What do you say?'

Roderick had begun to say that the loan he needed was more than the five hundred pounds held out as a distant prospect, when a clerk put his head round the door and said that Mr Hatherley was outside.

'Show him in by all means.' To Roderick he said, 'An American, big investor, likes to chance his arm, they call him Lucky Hatherley in his own country.' The American came in. 'This is my son-in-law Roderick Detling, heir to one of the most ancient baronetcies in the land.'

'I'm delighted to meet you, Mr Detling. The landed aristocracy of your country is something we just don't have in the States, and we miss that sense of tradition. Indeed, I'm a student of English history, and your family name is known to me. I believe the Detlings were honoured a long while back, by your Queen Elizabeth, isn't that so?'

'By Jove, yes, you're absolutely right. Though nowadays, you know, we're inclined to think it's all rather rot, about past history and so on. After all, it's what you do today that matters.'

'Never abandon your sense of tradition, it's a nation's most precious possession.' He turned to Blader. 'Now, governor, about these companies of which you've given me details. I've picked out three which would particularly interest me, International Tea Importers, Lever Chain Bicycles, and South African Rubber Developments. Do I understand you control these companies?'

'Not exactly. They're public companies floated with my help. South African Rubber has recently been reconstructed, by amalgamation with a couple of other companies that were under my wing. It now has the brightest possible prospects.'

Roderick rose to go, but Hatherley restrained him. 'Don't go, Mr Detling, unless you have to. We're talking finance, but there's nothing secret about it, and I'd like a chat when we've finished, if you can spare the time.'

The young man was not disinclined to stay. He had seen the governor in action before, and the operation was impressive, especially when he was selling a doubtful stock like South African Rubber, which Roderick knew that he would be eager to unload. But the procedure by which a particular stock was sold almost by understatement in the course of apparently praising another, was hardly necessary here, for the American had made up his mind. He was concerned only to get down the price and succeeded in doing so, although Roderick could see that the governor was happy with the result. After half an hour they had agreed figures.

'You're a hard man, Mr Hatherley, but I expected that. In fact, I like it.' Blader stretched out a hand across the desk, and Hatherley took it. 'My word's my bond, and I'm sure yours is too, but we'll have a bit of paper to say what we've agreed.

113

Then there's just the matter of settling up.'

'That will probably be in one week, at the most two. You understand, I don't keep that much ready cash on hand, and need to make certain arrangements. Payment will be in bonds or securities, similar to those I gave you before. Don't think this is the last deal we'll have, Lucky Hatherley will be back for more. But now that's business done, time for pleasure. If you're free, Mr Detling, I suggest we take a cab to Buszard's or Gunter's and have tea. I'd like to ask some questions about your family background, if I may. Genealogy is a subject that deeply interests me.'

Well, why not? There was nothing at all to occupy him at the Home Office, and this friendly American clearly had plenty of money. Perhaps he could be induced to put up some of it for research into the Detling family background or something of the kind. In any case, he seemed altogether too promising an acquaintance to drop. They had tea at Gunter's, for which Hatherley paid with money from a wallet stuffed with fivers, and Roderick talked about his parents, about Dolly and her politician husband, Nelly and her determination to attend art school, and about the way in which he himself was kept wretchedly short of the ready. The American listened, and asked an occasional question. Roderick found him extremely sympathetic.

'Talking about tradition and all that, of course I agree old customs should bally well be kept up, but how can a fellow do it when he's pretty well treated as a pauper by his father? I mean, it's a bit thick when your allowance is cut down, and you can't even borrow a few hundred because the girls have to be looked after. Of course, Dolly's married a chap who hasn't a penny, although he's a decent sort and I believe very clever, and I daresay Nelly will go the same way, but hang it, tradition

114

should mean that your son and heir comes first.'

He became aware that he had said more than he should have done, but Hatherley smiled and nodded, and didn't ask awkward or impertinent questions. He was a remarkably decent fellow for an American, and when they parted Roderick said that he would like Hatherley to come to dinner one evening. The American said that he could always be found at the Savoy.

8 *The Murder*

'It's a mess, sir,' said the young constable who had been standing in the doorway. 'It fair turned me up.'

'You get used to these things, lad,' Inspector Moss said as they trudged heavy-footed up the stairs. 'Though I know what you mean. The first time I saw a dead woman my stomach turned over. Nothing out of the way, you understand, she looked peaceful enough, but because it was the fair sex I could hardly look at her. If it'd been a man, I wouldn't have batted an eyelid.' With no change of tone he said, 'Somebody been talking to the other people in the house, I hope.'

'Sergeant Tranter, sir, speaking to them now.'

'That's good, though I doubt if he'll get much. See no evil, hear no evil, that's their motto.' They reached the top floor. Moss went into the room, and stood still for a few seconds taking it in. 'I see what you mean, constable. A mess, and no mistake.'

There was a lot of blood about. It had splashed one of the walls, gone on to the nearby canvases, and extended across the floor to the dingy curtain that had separated the sleeping area from the rest of the room. This curtain had been pulled down, and lay half across the table which had on it the dead man's painting materials, an empty bottle of beer, and a plate containing part of a saveloy and a half-eaten potato. Two glasses had contained beer, but one of them had been knocked over, and beer stains were mixed with the blood. Blood spots on one canvas were particularly noticeable because most of the picture was painted in a virulent green.

The body itself was sprawled on the floor beside the table.

The man was fully dressed, in an old shirt and trousers, with a painter's smock over them. His head had been savagely beaten, and a poker covered with blood and hair lay a couple of feet from the body. Moss was a big, heavy man, but he dropped down beside the body smoothly enough, turning the head to examine the injuries. When he got up he dusted the knees of his trousers, and looked at the unmade bed with its grimy blankets, and the rest of the furniture, two shelves for books and the rickety old chest of drawers. The books had been pulled from the shelves and the drawers emptied of their clothing, which was strewn around the floor.

'Anything occur to you, constable?'

'Yes, sir. Whoever killed him was looking for something.'

'So much is obvious. I meant, did anything strike you about the look of the body?'

'Only that it's all such a mess, sir, whoever did it must have blood on his clothes.'

'Yes, probably, though I've known cases where there was blood all around and the murderer's shirt was white as if it had just come from the laundry. I had one or two other things in mind. The crime was unpremeditated, the killer didn't bring a weapon with him, just picked up what was handy. The two men probably knew each other, since the dead man poured his visitor a glass of beer. The time can be pretty well fixed by the food. This kind of stuff comes from a cooked meat shop, no means of cooking in the room as you'll have noticed, and by checking on the ones round about we should be able to find out when Settleby bought it. It's plain the caller interrupted his meal. And if you'll look at the way the blows were delivered you'll see they were struck from behind, and go diagonally from left to right. So the murderer was right-handed, and Settleby wasn't expecting trouble or he wouldn't have turned his back. Keep your eyes open, you'll be surprised what you can spot.'

'Yes, sir. You'll find what was in his pockets laid out the other end of the table.'

Moss nodded and looked. There were a few coppers, a key, a rag which had been used to wipe off paint, and two bits of paper. One was a receipt for fifteen pounds signed 'Hugo Yarborough', and the other contained a name and address which made Moss raise his eyebrows.

'Here's Sergeant Tranter. And somebody with him from the sound of it.'

The sergeant was large and ponderous. He had with him a lank-haired woman.

'This here alleges she's the dead man's wife, sir.'

'I don't know what you mean by that. We were married ten years ago for better or worse, and mostly it's been worse.' She saw the body. 'Oh, Eustace, you poor devil. Who did it, who did that to him?'

'That's what we'd like to know,' the Inspector said. 'You lived here with him? Why weren't you here last night?'

'We had a row two or three days ago and I moved out, went to stay with a pal of mine. It's happened before, he got quarrelsome when he had drink in him. I'd have come back, he knew that. I always came back.'

'What was the row about?'

'He was having a show of his paintings, first for years, and I got a bit sarky about it, said it was the money I got as a model kept us going, he never sold any pictures. Though he did sell one not long ago, we had a party. Anyway, he caught me a whack on the cheek, and I cleared off.' She saw the drawers emptied of clothes beside the bed. 'Did whoever killed him do that? Eustace never had anything worth a brass farthing, nor me either.'

119

'Somebody thought different. The question is, did they find what they were looking for?'

The sergeant coughed. 'The witness alleges she spent last night with a woman named Haines, who also says she's an artist's model. Haines confirms her story. Then the witness alleges she heard of Settleby's death this morning, and came round here. Haines says she can provide other witnesses who will say they were in the Fitzroy public house until closing time. This has not yet been corroborated.'

'For Christ's sake, you don't think I killed him? Why, I loved the poor bastard.'

'Mrs Settleby, I'm sorry to distress you,' Moss said. 'Constable, cover the body with that curtain. The doctor will be here shortly, and you'll understand the body can't be moved until he has seen it. Now, just two or three more questions. You say your husband sold a picture. Do you know who bought it?'

'No. Only that he was suddenly very flush, and we had a party. With champagne.'

'Do you know the name Yarborough?'

'Yes. He's the dealer who's putting on Eustace's exhibition.'

'Your husband apparently paid him fifteen pounds. The receipt was in his pocket.'

She stared at him, and then laughed. 'So he was paying for his pictures to be shown. I might have known it. Poor Eustace, poor bloody useless Eustace.'

'You have no idea where he could have got such an amount of money?'

'None in the world. He sometimes had a few bob in his pocket. I don't even know where that came from, he used to say he'd done a job helping out with a bit of stage scenery painting, things like that. And he'd had more money lately, I'll say that.'

120

'How much would he have sold a picture for?'

'He'd have been lucky if it was more than a tenner, probably less. I wondered where the money came from for the party, he must have struck it rich somehow or other, these last few weeks.'

The Inspector nodded. He mentioned the name on the other piece of paper, but Laura Settleby had never heard of it. Then he looked round at the canvases.

'So this is what his paintings were like. I'd never seen one. I'm not surprised he couldn't sell them.'

'You mean you knew him?' she asked in surprise.

'Oh yes,' Moss said. 'I knew him. That's why I'm here.'

9 *Questions and Answers*

'The name is unknown to you?' the Inspector asked.

'Entirely unknown. Frankly, Inspector, I haven't any idea at all why my name should be in his pocket.' Bernard sat at ease in the drawing room, one leg crossed over the other. Moss, opposite him, was bolt upright, bowler hat on his knee. The upper part of his face, with its thick drooping moustache and heavily pouched eyes, seemed to belong to a bloodhound, the formidable thrusting jaw below to a bulldog.

'You didn't happen to buy a picture from him? Or to buy one of his pictures from an art dealer?'

'I certainly did not. In fact, I can tell you nothing at all. And since I shall continue to repeat those words if you ask me anything further about this unknown man, I think I should return to my correspondence and leave you to find more informative witnesses.'

The Inspector did not stir. He turned his bowler hat round gently, and said, 'I do have a few more questions, sir. I don't think I shall be wasting your time by putting them. You see, Mr Ross, I am employed at the Special Department of Scotland Yard's Criminal Investigation Department. Possibly you may know that our job is to keep watch on all political criminals and possible suspects, Anarchists, Fenians and so on. Particularly Fenians. I expect you've heard of the Special Department.'

'Yes, I have heard of it. Go on.'

'One particular job I have to do is to keep track of any Irish over in this country from the States whom we think may be likely to cause trouble, by dynamite explosions in public

123

buildings – which as you're aware, has been attempted and even carried out in recent years – or by attacks on public figures such as politicians, or even the Royal family. Those are my particular duties.'

'Very interesting, Inspector, but hardly my affair.'

'Perhaps not, sir. It will come as no surprise to you that we use informants, and indeed place considerable reliance on them. Settleby was one of those informants. He was often at the Anarchist Club off Tottenham Court Road, he met a lot of students and young people, he had a good many Irish acquaintances. I had an arrangement by which I met him every couple of weeks or so at a pub near Scotland Yard. He gave me whatever bits of information he had picked up, and I paid him for them.'

'There you are. That's where the money came from, the money you said he had paid to the art dealer to put on his show.'

Moss gave a bulldog's grin, showing a mouthful of yellow teeth. 'Oh no, sir. A pound was the most I ever gave him, and mostly it was a few shillings. Our masters aren't lavish. So you will see why I was interested when I found your name and address in his pocket. It looks as though that stuff about selling a picture was just a tale, and his money came from somewhere else.'

'I understand. Had he told you anything recently that was of importance?'

'He might have done, yes. Hard to be sure. He was useful, but not reliable.'

'Is it not more than possible, even likely, that one of his Fenian acquaintances learned that he was passing on information about them, and killed him?'

'Obviously a possibility, Mr Ross, yes. It doesn't explain

why your name was in his pocket. A few days ago, to be precise on Thursday of last week, you entertained three Irish gentlemen here. Were you aware that they are all members of the terrorist organisation called the Irish Republican Brotherhood, and that in the United States two of them were tried for murder?'

Bernard Ross said sharply, 'You have been watching my house. I regard that as intolerable.'

'No, sir. We are keeping an eye on Mr. Devas and his friends to discover their intentions, which may of course be perfectly innocent. Accordingly we know that they visited your house. You haven't answered my question.'

'I don't admit your right to ask it, but I will answer. Yes, I knew that Devas and his friends were members of the I.R.B., and that they had been on trial. I knew also that they had been acquitted. They asked to see me. I am a Member of Parliament, much concerned with the Irish question. It was my duty to see them and listen to them. Mr Morley or Mr MacMurdo would have done the same.'

'And what was the subject of your conversation, sir? Or let me put it another way. Did you discuss any matters that would concern me as a member of the Special Department?'

Bernard picked up a lacquered case from the table, opened it. 'Do you indulge, Inspector? I find an occasional Abdulla very soothing to the spirit.' Moss shook his head and sat patiently while a match was put to the oval tube. 'They tried to bribe me,' Bernard said, smiling.

'How's that, sir? *Bribe* you?'

'I don't wonder that you're surprised. After luncheon I took them into my study, and the suggestion was made there.'

'You mean that money was offered if you gave them information? It was said in so many words?'

125

'Not quite. Devas was their spokesman. He said that they understood from my speeches that I had sympathy with the Republican cause. They themselves would probably be returning to the United States shortly, but others in sympathy with the cause would remain here, and it would be of the greatest help to them to know details of government policy on Ireland, and of the official attitude towards the I.R.B. He went on to hint broadly that they knew I was not a man of means, and said that the Brotherhood in the States had very considerable funds and was accustomed to paying handsomely for any information given to them. I told them that I was not in the business of selling information, and showed them the door. The courtesies of gentlemanly behaviour were preserved throughout, not an impolite word was said, and indeed I found the little episode as good as a scene in a play. But perhaps you are not a theatregoer.'

The Inspector ignored the last sentence. 'I don't understand why they should have approached you.'

'Neither do I.' He blew a smoke ring. 'It seemed to me that I sensed a kind of reserve in Devas – the other two hardly spoke – as though there was something he had expected me to understand, or perhaps as if my reactions were not what he expected. But it was an impression, no more.'

'I don't take much stock in impressions, sir. I prefer facts.'

'Very worthy of you, Inspector.'

'I'd like to tell you some facts. On four occasions in the last year we've received information about dynamite explosions planned to blow up parts of public buildings in this country. One was to plant a bomb in the Stock Exchange. You'll understand that we work closely with the Irish section at the Home Office. I'm not in a position to give you details, I'll only say that twice we found dynamite, but we drew a blank as far as

126

catching any of them was concerned. What do you make of that?'

'Perhaps your men made themselves conspicuous too soon. Or, in the cases where you found nothing at all, perhaps your information was faulty.'

'Or perhaps somebody tipped off the dynamiters.'

'That is a possibility, of course, although I should have thought a remote one. And now, Inspector, I hope you will agree that I have been patient in answering your questions, and I must ask you to forgive me. I hear my wife at the door, back from doing good works in Whitechapel. And here she is. My dear, this is Detective Inspector Moss from Scotland Yard, who is on the track of our Irish acquaintances, whom he has been watching so closely that he was aware of their visit here, and perhaps can even tell us what we ate for luncheon. He also wondered if I had bought a picture from an artist who has just been murdered.'

Dolly had come straight into the drawing room, wearing her hat and coat. She looked from one to the other in bewilderment.

'Name of Eustace Settleby,' Moss said as he got up. 'Had a piece of paper in his pocket with your husband's name on it. You've not heard the name, Mrs Ross? Ah well. No doubt there's an explanation somewhere. I must thank you for sparing me your valuable time, Mr Ross.'

With that he was gone, blue-overcoated, stiff-backed, his bloodhound or bulldog face solemn under his bowler. He had not been satisfied by the answers to his questions, and was not convinced that Mr Bernard Ross, M.P., had been candid with him. At the same time it was obviously true that if the Irish had learned of information being passed on to the Yard by Settleby, they might have killed him. But who could have told them?

10 *Visits to Whitechapel*

Gertrude demurred at the idea of inviting to dinner an American they didn't know from Adam. It would be necessary to ask other people too, she pointed out, and since he was in London unaccompanied by a wife, a single woman must be there to make up the numbers. The whole thing would mean trouble and expense, and wasn't Roderick always asking her to avoid expense? Surely it would be quite sufficient to ask this total stranger to tea?

So Mr Hatherley was asked to tea. He ate his sandwiches and little cakes with every sign of pleasure, said that afternoon tea was one of those great English institutions that made the country what it was, showed interest in little Billy and said that he was the image of his beautiful mother except perhaps for having his father's nose, and altogether conducted himself so agreeably that Gertrude afterwards said he was really extremely gentlemanly. The two men went for a stroll around Kensington after tea, and walked further than Roderick had intended, so that he realised that they were near his sister's home. When he suggested that they might call, Hatherley said that he would be delighted. The door was opened by Lizzie, who told them her master and mistress were both out. On the way back to his own home Roderick brought the conversation not exactly to his own need of money, which he felt might have been tactless, but to his interest in Hatherley's attempt to break into the English market.

'You couldn't have a better guide than the governor. Of course I work with him very closely. If I can be of help in any way, you know you can call on me.'

'That's mighty good of you, and it could be I'll take you up on it. I don't plan to stay in this country more than a few months, and when I go I shall need someone to keep an eye on my affairs. I reckon the governor can't spare the time, and if I thought I could call on you for that service it would be a weight off my mind. And if you wouldn't be insulted, I'd be glad if you would accept a fee for the service.'

Roderick said that he would be delighted to be of use, and did not deny that some kind of remuneration would be acceptable. Hatherley expressed himself proud to be associated with the ancient name of Detling. They parted on the best of terms.

Dolly returned half an hour after her brother and Hatherley had called. Bernard had said that he would be at the House late, so she settled down at the desk in her own little work room to complete some of the forms that were an inevitable accompaniment of Association work. She had not been there five minutes when Lizzie came in without knocking.

'That toff I told you about, he's been here.'

'Lizzie, please remember to knock before you come into a room. Now, take a breath and tell me what you're talking about.'

'I'm sorry.' The girl's eyes were glittering with excitement. 'Remember when you came down and fetched me, we met Fred coming into the place where we lived as we was coming out, and I told you there'd been a toff down to see 'im – him – wore a topper and shook hands with Fred. Well, it was that one who came, along with your brother. Left this card, I've just taken it from the hall. Spoke in a funny sort of way, not like English.'

Dolly read the name on the card. 'I think, from his name, he is probably American. Are you sure he was the same? One gentleman in a top hat looks very much like another.'

130

'I'm sure,' Lizzie said earnestly. 'Tisn't often we get toffs like him coming down our way, so I noticed him particular. And then he's such a gentleman, dressed up to the nines, and so handsome with such a nice smile, you couldn't mistake him. He was the one who came with a gentleman said he was your brother, truly, madam. I'm not mistaken.'

Dolly looked again at the card, with its unknown name. Here was one more minor mystery to add to the others like Bernard's readiness to receive the revolutionary Irishmen, and the business about the man who had been killed. At least she could investigate this one.

'I have to go to Whitechapel tomorrow,' she said. 'You shall come with me, Lizzie. It's time you saw your mother and father. And we can pay a call on Fred.'

The following day was a Friday, and the first snow of winter was falling. Mr Modkin was talking, or rather listening, to a lady wearing a fur-trimmed purple coat surmounted by a fur hat with ostrich plumes. Mary Tracy was interviewing a girl and her mother was at the other side of the room. Dolly and Lizzie sat down on small wooden chairs to wait.

'I dismissed the gel immediately,' said the lady in the fur hat. 'She was lazy, impertinent and a drunkard. I really don't know why you should have sent me such a gel.'

Mr Modkin's Adam's apple moved frantically up and down. 'I am extremely sorry, Mrs – um – very sorry indeed that Jane –'

'Her name was Jenny. Perhaps you sent the wrong gel.'

'Jenny, of course, not by any means the wrong girl, quite the right, um, the girl we, um, meant to send. As I say I am very sorry she should have been, um, unsatisfactory but I fear Mrs, um, that allowances have to be made for an unfortunate background. There may always be one bad apple in a um –'

131

'One does what one can to help the cause, but impertinence and drunkenness together is too much.' The ostrich plumes wavered. Mr. Modkin muttered something which could not be heard. 'That's as may be, and I understand your problems, but they are no excuse for laziness and impertinence. I will give a trial to *one* more of your gels, and I shall expect you to send one who is clean, industrious, respectful and *sober*.' She rose and swept out of the office. The mother and child with Mary Tracy watched, awestruck. Mr Modkin smiled feebly at Dolly.

'Mrs, um, Ross, good morning. What is the problem with our young friend here?'

'There is no problem. This is Lizzie, Lizzie Comstock, who is working for me as a parlourmaid. She is giving every satisfaction. I have brought her down to visit her parents, and thought you might like to see her.'

'Indeed.' Mr Modkin beamed at Lizzie, and scratched his chin. 'You are looking quite different today, Lizzie, from when I last saw you. The difference is an, um, improvement, if I may say so. Are you happy in your position?'

Lizzie took her time to consider this, and then said 'It's all right.'

'Splendid. Now, will you just register with Mrs Tracy so that she may mark your card. I am delighted to hear that you are getting on well.' He leaned across the table and extended his long dry hand to Lizzie, who touched it with her small one.

'Wouldn't like to work for that one with the feathers,' she said when they were outside. 'I wouldn't stop there, I'd run away.'

'Then it's just as well you work for me, isn't it? Will you be pleased to see your family?'

'Don't know. S'pose so.'

Purchase Court was no better than Dolly had remembered,

and as she entered the house the stench struck her more intensely than before. The door of the top front room was partly open, and when they went in the scene seemed hardly to have changed from Dolly's previous visit. Lizzie's mother sat sewing as she had done before, Lizzie's sister was asleep on one of the beds, and the two boys were making paper darts which they threw at each other. The bed on which Lizzie's father had slept, however, was empty.

Lizzie said 'Hello, mum.' The woman put down her sewing, came across and embraced her, then stood back and looked at her daughter.

'You don't half look different, Liz. So smart.' Lizzie was wearing a dark blue woollen coat that Dolly had bought her, with a matching hat. 'How's she getting on?'

'She's settled down very well.' Dolly was conscious of the inadequacy of the phrase, but what else could she say? 'Isn't that so, Lizzie?'

'S'all right.' Lizzie wore woollen gloves, which she kept pulling on and off.

'Say hallo to Liz.'

The boys looked at their sister. 'Wotcher wearin' those duds for, Liz?' one of them asked. 'You don't 'arf look funny.'

'She got 'em for me.' Lizzie jabbed a finger towards Dolly. 'Where's 'e gone?'

'Down the docks,' her mother answered. 'Steady work he's had, the last couple of weeks.' There was a silence, which Dolly did not know how to break. 'You do look smart, no two ways about it.' Another silence. 'It was good of you to bring Liz round.'

'It's part of our work, to bring girls back to see their parents. Shall I leave Lizzie with you for an hour or two?'

'Better not, might get her clothes dirty. Not but what I'm

pleased to know she's getting on all right, but she don't belong with us now. Give your mum a kiss, Liz, then you'd best be off.'

When they were going down the stairs Lizzie said, 'I don't want to come here no more. Do I have to?'

'Not if you don't want to. I can come to see your mother, and tell her how you're getting on. You were going to show me Fred's room, remember?'

'Next floor down. This one.'

Dolly knocked. The door looked as if it were suffering from a skin disease in the form of unpleasant little bubbles and crusts where the paint had partly worn away, and the disease seemed to have infected the woman who opened it. She was obviously getting ready to go out, and her clothes were gaudy but fairly clean. Her face, however, was pitted by the remains of smallpox, and also marked by small boils or large pimples. She looked at them. 'What the 'ell do you want?'

'We were looking for your husband, Mr Harrison.' Lizzie had told her that was Fred's surname.

'You were, were you? Well, 'e ain't 'ere, and I'm off out.' There was a smell about her that Dolly recognised as gin. The woman picked up a hat trimmed with bright ribbons, and closed the door.

'Mrs Harrison, it's me, Liz.'

The woman peered down in the semi-darkness. 'So it is, I'd never 'a' known you. Your ma told me you'd gorn off somewhere to work. And 'oo's she?'

'She only wants to talk to Fred. We're trying to find someone, see, and we think Fred knows where he might be.'

'Well, I dunno.' She went down the stairs, swaying slightly, and they followed her. 'I s'pose it's orl right, and I don't much care if it ain't. Fred's working steady just now, a place by

134

Roper's dye factory. If you see 'im, say I'll be in the Goat and Compasses. Ta ta for now, Liz.' Her feet tapped on the cobbles as she turned left out of Purchase Court. Lizzie led Dolly in the opposite direction.

The snow was falling thickly now, powdering the ground, making even these grimy alleys look faintly romantic. Lizzie took Dolly's hand and began to talk.

'That Ruby Harrison, my ma says she's no good, always on the drink and brings back men when Fred ain't there. Fred'd be better off without her, ma says, she's just a tart.' Although Dolly was in favour of free speech, she felt she should have rebuked Lizzie for these words, but did not know quite how to do so. 'I don't want to go back. It ain't no good. Back 'ome I mean.'

'I'm sorry if it upset you. I said you needn't go back again.'

'Don't matter about upsetting me. It just ain't no good, that's all.'

They had been threading a way through the alleys, and now came to Commercial Road, which was full of stalls and dray carts. They crossed over, and entered an area where the alleys were replaced by recognisable streets with narrow pavements. Dolly asked if Lizzie knew where they were going.

'I know the dye factory, we all do, it makes such a stink, can't yer smell it? Just round the corner, there it is.'

They were in a narrow street, with small cottages on the left-hand side of it, and on the right a long low building that might have been called a shed, with a chimney at the back from which a plume of smoke rose straight into the leaden sky. The name Roper was printed along the side of the shed. The smell was rather like burning rubber, quite different from that in Purchase Court but much less unpleasant. They came to the entrance of the factory, a double gate near which an elderly

135

man sat in a cabin resembling a slightly enlarged dog kennel.
'Mrs Harrison said a place by the dye factory, but where do
you suppose that can be?'
'I'll arsk him.' Lizzie went up to the dog kennel. The man
inside looked out at them through a very small glass window.
She tapped on the door, but he took no notice. She shouted
'We're looking for Fred, Fred Harrison.'

The man opened the door a few inches. 'Down there.
Second on the left.'

'Do you mean he's part of the dyeing works?' Dolly asked.

'Best ask him.'

'Why didn't you open the door when we knocked?'

'Too cold,' the man said, and shut the door again.

'Fred won't be working for Roper's,' Lizzie said. 'They've
got a lot of empty sheds down here, they rent 'em to people
who want to start up business, store things and that. Mum
worked for a dressmaker down here once.'

They picked their way over muddy, deeply rutted ground, in
which empty cans lay around, together with broken cart
wheels and other bits of waggons. The second shed on the left
was a black painted structure about thirty feet long and half
that width, with one small window at the end.

'You know a lot, Lizzie. Where would I be without you?'

Lizzie looked at her with one of the rare smiles that transformed her face. 'I was born here, warn't I? Let's have a look
through that window. 'Oo's this?'

As they approached the window a man came out of the shed
and walked towards them. He was a thick-necked young fellow
with hair cropped close to his head, and he wore a set of
workmen's overalls over a striped flannel shirt open at the
neck. He said to Dolly, in a voice of mock politeness, 'What
are you looking for down here, ma'am, may I ask?'

136

'We want to speak to Fred Harrison.'

As she spoke the words, Dolly felt the absurdity of what she was doing. When she saw Fred Harrison, what had she to say to him, beyond some vague tale about a servant girl having identified a man who called at her house as somebody seen previously in the East End? Whatever would Bernard say to her if he knew about it?

'Do you now? And might I enquire the nature of your business?'

'I should prefer to tell Mr Harrison himself.'

'You would, would you?' He was grinning as he came close to Dolly. He smelt of beer and onions. 'I'll tell you what *I* should prefer, shall I? I should prefer that you slung your hook out of here pronto, and took this brat with you. Wait a minute, don't I know you?' He took Lizzie by the arm with one hand, and with the other pushed up her chin so that he could see her face. 'My word, if it ain't Lizzie that used to live in the same house as Fred. Ain't you dressed up like a dog's dinner?'

'And I know *you.*' Lizzie jerked away from him. 'You're Jack Whitehouse.'

Still grinning, the young man bent down, put his hand to the ground, and came up with a handful of mud. 'Be a pity to spoil that nice blue coat, wouldn't it. Don't you think so, ma'am?'

Threats of any kind made Dolly angry. Now she told Lizzie to go and find a policeman. The girl gave her a despairing glance, and the young man roared with laughter.

'She'd have a long walk. You'll find as many bobbies down this way as you do pearly kings in the Ritz. Now, I don't know who you are or what you bleedin' want with old Fred, but you'll just have to take Jack Whitehouse's word for it that he's busy and don't want to see you. So skedaddle, vamoose, make yourself scarce, or I'll have to do something to show you as how you ain't wanted.'

137

Dolly had been in other dingy parts of the East End without ever feeling frightened, but under the leaden sky, in the desolate landscape of dilapidated sheds and bits of rusting machinery, with snowflakes falling, she knew that she was in physical danger and that something terrible might happen, something which had no place in the ordered world that she knew. The bruiser, still grinning, held out his palm upwards to catch the flakes, so that they settled on the mud. The gesture was somehow decisive. She said, 'Come, Lizzie,' and they turned away. Behind them she heard the young man's mocking laughter.

Nothing was said until they had passed the man in the dog kennel, and were hurrying along the road. Then Lizzie spoke.

'He's a nasty piece of work, that Jack Whitehouse. My mum says 'e's got a record as long as your arm. Why d'you suppose he wouldn't let us see Fred?'

'I don't know.'

'Shall we come down again?'

'Perhaps I might come alone. I don't like being beaten by someone like Jack Whitehouse.'

'*Madam.*' Lizzie's hand tightened on her arm. 'There he is. Over the road.'

Dolly had been walking head down, but now she looked up, and felt the snow on her face. A man wearing a dark ankle-length coat was hurrying along on the other side of the road. He wore a curly-brimmed bowler and had his head down, so that she could see little of his features except that he wore a moustache. As she watched he crossed the road, and entered the gate of the dye factory. Could Lizzie be right about the identification, and if she was, what did the man want with Fred Harrison? And why should she suppose that his activities had any connection with Bernard? To this last question she could

138

give no reasonable answer. Later she told her husband only that she had taken Lizzie to see her family, and that the visit had not been a success. Bernard said that he was not surprised.

It was another week before she could nerve herself to make a second call in Purchase Court, and she recoiled when the door of Harrison's room was opened by Jack Whitehouse. He looked blank for a moment, then grinned.

'If it isn't Lady Ladida, who wanted to see Fred. You don't give up, do you?'

She tried to peer past him. 'Where is he?'

'Where he always is when he's got a few quid in his pocket, taken his tart down to Margate to spend it. And I'm looking after things for him while he's gone.'

'I don't believe you.'

'Come in and see for yourself.' He held the door wide. A young woman, hardly more than a girl, sat up in bed naked from the waist up, and began to use such foul language, to Dolly and Jack Whitehouse, who lolled grinning beside the door, that Dolly fled.

She went to the dye factory and tried the door of the shed that Harrison was supposed to have been using, but it was locked. The man in the enlarged dog kennel said that the people who had been working in the shed had given it up and gone, he couldn't say where.

And that was the end of the Whitechapel trail.

11 *Investigation and Promotion*

Detective Inspector Moss had a low opinion of the Irish
section and of its chief, Mr Vincent, who spent most of the day
at his club, and in the office was known colloquially as the
Dormouse. Moss had some respect for Patterwick's filing
system, however, and because of this asked the young man to
come and see him at the Yard. The Inspector's room there was
small and bare, furnished with a table and two hard chairs,
decorated by photographs of the police sports, in which Moss
had been a member of the tug-of-war team ten years ago. He
was fond of saying that you find criminals in the streets, not in
an office, but still there were times when he had to sit down at
a desk, and this was one of them. Patterwick had brought
along the files relating to Devas, O'Brien and Flaherty, and
they were bulky. They contained, however, no obvious links
with Eustace Settleby.

'The devil of it is that they knew him, and knew him well,'
Moss said. 'His widow, the one who calls herself an artist's
model, testifies to that. Do you suppose that Settleby was playing a double game, giving me scraps of information about the
Irish, and passing on news to them about our activities? He
was rogue enough for it. I've told you already that there's been
more than one occasion in recent months when we've foiled
the plot but missed the dynamiters. We can't put all that down
to our three new Irish friends, they've been here only a short
while and if they're to be believed intend to leave before long.
They're here for a reason, though, and I'd dearly like to know
what it is.'

'You have men watching them?'

141

'You bet your life. They've been making a regular tour, the Tower and St Paul's, Hampton Court Palace, British Museum and so on. They're always together, so they're easy to follow. They're great tipplers. At a pub by the Tower they got into conversation with a couple of Beefeaters and stood them I don't know how many rounds, then down in Woolwich they did the same with some young soldiers, poured drink into them till it ran out of their ears, so my men said.'

'Trying to get information about the Tower and Woolwich Barracks?'

'Possibly. Or it may be they're on a spree, flinging around the money they've got from America. I've known some who talked about the cause all the time they were filling their bellies and throwing money around like a man with ten hands. This lot are gamblers, Devas especially, and he seems to have all the money in the world in his pocket. So they may be over here on a spree, or any one of those places they've visited might be a target. I'd lay a bet they're trying to pull the wool over my eyes one way or another, but I'll have them, Mr Patterwick, I'll have them'

'Do you know what they were doing when Settleby was killed?'

'Doesn't help. We've pretty well fixed the time of his death. The Doctor says it was between eight and ten in the evening, and soon after eight he went out to a cooked meat shop and bought a meal which was only partly eaten. Our three villains were supposed to be in their lodgings at Clerkenwell, but it would have been easy for one or more of them to slip out. What do you know about a gentleman named Bernard Ross?'

Paul's eyelids fluttered. 'The Member of Parliament? Nothing at all, although his brother-in-law, Roderick Detling, is a friend of mine.'

'You don't keep a file on him?' Paul shook his head. 'You know he's concerned with Irish affairs, always making speeches about Home Rule. If they asked my opinion, which they don't, I'd say he spouted a lot of rubbish. You should have a file on a man like that.'

Paul Patterwick looked concerned. 'I couldn't start one on my own account, any more than I could on Mr Gladstone. If you felt that there should be a file you would have to take it up with Mr Vincent. I don't think it would be looked on favourably.'

Moss snorted. 'I daresay not. The point about Mr Bernard Ross is, he comes from the States. Been over here a few years now, but said to hail from just outside Chicago, and brought up by an uncle in the city, so I read in a newspaper not long ago. I'd like to check on his background there.'

'Do you really mean that you suspect him of being mixed up with the Brotherhood? That seems very far-fetched.'

'I've known more unlikely things to be true. But I don't mean anything at present, I just want to check on Ross's background. I could send a cable myself to the Chicago police department, but the quickest way might be if you cabled one of your agents. I want to know what work he did with his uncle, who his associates were, when he left Chicago, whether he or his family had any connection with the Brotherhood, the Clan-na-Gael, or any other of the Anarchists over there.' To the Inspector, all bombers and dynamiters were Anarchists, no matter what their political beliefs. 'If you could do that I'd be obliged. It would save time, maybe, with Christmas coming up, if the reply was sent straight to me at Scotland Yard. And keep it under your hat. This is between you and me. There may be nothing in it, nothing at all.'

Paul understood that this request had been the detective's

143

real purpose in asking to see him. He agreed to send the cable, rose to go, then hesitated.

'Perhaps I should mention one thing, Inspector. I'm going down to stay with the Detlings at Christmas, and Ross will be there.'

'A nod's as good as a wink to a blind horse,' Moss said heartily. 'Glad you told me. I'd be glad to know anything you can find out from him, just by chatting like. I know it would be infra dig, as they say, to ask a gentleman to spy on his friends, but it's nice to know someone in the camp. And if you learn anything you think I should know, send a telegram. If I'm not here, they always know where to find me.'

With that Paul gathered up his files and left. The Inspector had not told him of the link between Ross and Settleby implied in the paper found in the dead man's pocket. He did not distrust young Patterwick, but simply saw no reason to pass on information which he could keep to himself.

Eustace Settleby's death was hardly even a nine days' wonder. The Yarborough gallery fulfilled their obligation by putting on a show of Settleby's paintings, but although the notoriety brought in a good many visitors, the gallery sold only one painting. The murder was talked about at the Slade by the students who had known Settleby, and one or two who had seen him on the day of his death were interviewed by the police. It was agreed that he had been his usual self, boasting and quarrelsome, and much preoccupied with his coming show. Nelly went to see the show with Charlie Bangs.

'They're such glaring colours. I don't like them any better than I did in his studio,' she said. 'I mean, he talked about Turner, but he didn't use all these fierce reds and blues, did he?'

'Turner used everything,' her companion said absently. 'Mind you, I think Eustace had some quality or other. At least he wasn't a grey man. Or a grey painter. I know he was rude to you, and there was no excuse for that.'

'I didn't mind, although I didn't like the way he kept saying I was middle class. He seemed to dislike the whole family.' There was a bench in the centre of the room, and she sat down on it. 'Charlie, I'm bored with living at home. I think we should elope.'

'You've said that before. And I've told you, there's nothing wrong with marriage, with getting married in the usual way I mean. Except –' He hesitated.

'You see,' she said triumphantly. 'There is something.'

'Just my family. We're comfortable, not rich, and my father expects me to follow him into the business. I'm just being allowed my fling.'

'Then why not live together, wouldn't that be part of the fling? It would show *him* who's middle class.' She put out her tongue at the pictures.

'Nelly! I believe you're saying this to lay the ghost of what Eustace said about you. The truth is, whether we married or not, I wouldn't be able to support you.'

'Does that matter?'

'Well, doesn't it?'

She wrinkled her nose. 'I'll tell you something that puzzles me. How is it that you paint these pictures that are so – that sometimes make me shiver, and yet you're socially a very conventional person. It's as though you were two people.'

'Perhaps I am. Perhaps you've never seen Mr Hyde.'

'I'll tell you something else if you look away.' He did so, gazing at a painting of bulbous shapes in cobalt blue and mustard. 'I might be able to arrange for us to have adjoining rooms at Chadderley.'

*

Blader contemplated the articles on his desk with pleasure. There they were, forty of them, the first sample batch of Everlasting Pens. In appearance they were chastely black like most fountain pens, with a gold clip. There was a genuine guaranteed nine-carat rolled-gold nib. Unscrew the top, and instead of the rubber sac that grew hard and inflexible with use, there was the thin sleek tube which would provide ink for a year. The pen would be in full production early in the New Year, and they would launch an advertising campaign after Christmas. When the Everlasting Pen had driven all other fountain pens off the market there would no longer be that lingering doubt, in his own mind as well as in the heads of other City people, about his solvency. He was still using the pen he had been given by Gabriel Harris, and the ink flowed as easily as ever. The rest of this sample would be distributed in the office, to friends, to the party at Chadderley. He liked the idea of impressing the party at Chadderley.

In the meantime he made a start by giving one to Duncan J. Hatherley. The American wrote with it, observed its refusal to smudge, obediently shook it in an attempt to make one of the ink blots to which ordinary fountain pens were prone, and nodded his handsome head in appreciation.

'I'd say you're on a winner here, governor. What's your price?'

Blader had been contemplating the row of pens with admiration. 'What's that?'

'I take it you're floating a company, and I'd like to get in on it. I asked what price you'll be putting on the shares.'

The financier saw that his enthusiasm had betrayed him. He should have remembered Hatherley's readiness to buy almost anything he saw or was told about. He put genuine

146

regret into his voice. 'I'm sorry. The inventor's keeping most of the shares under his own control, and although I've got a few of the rest, they won't be going on the market. We may put them on the market later on, if more capital is needed, but frankly I doubt it.'

'You're saying this little article will be a success from the word go, and I believe you're right. It's one of the cutest things I ever saw. Well now, if I'm not going to be a shareholder in Everlasting Pens, let's get down to cases. Here's my shopping list.'

It was a list that would have made the governor whistle, if he had been given to showing his emotions in that way. Hatherley was taking large parcels, not only of the three companies he had picked out, but of others as well. The payment, as before, was in bonds drawn on Rothschild's. Blader could have told the American that if he made money on all, or even most, of the shareholdings he would deserve his name of Lucky Hatherley. Instead he beamed all over his broad face, said that he admired American enterprise, and that the occasion called for a celebration in bubbly. Half an hour later they were still drinking Veuve Clicquot, and smoking Corona Coronas.

Dolly read extracts from Bernard's speech in *The Times*. He had told her that agreement to the recall of Parliament in early November, after the longest session ever recorded, lasting as it had from January to early September, had been given to the opposition on the understanding that no contentious matters like the Irish question should be raised.

Accordingly, several days had been spent in discussing the Parish Councils Bill, and it would be succeeded by the Employers' Liability Bill.

147

She did not understand how Bernard had managed to find a chance to attack the House of Lords but he had done so, in what was called in the newspaper a brief but brilliant speech. 'The House of Lords is a club of Tory landlords which in its gilded chamber has disposed of the welfare of people with almost exclusive regard to the interests of a class ... a great dead weight of prejudice and bigotry resting upon the back of a nation ... since they are immovable by discussion and impervious to reason, in the end it will be necessary to drive these bigots from their hereditary and antiquated entrenchments, not by argument or by reason, but by force.' *The Times* Parliamentary correspondent commented that 'Mr John Morley could be observed nodding his head gravely at these words, while the Prime Minister himself, hand cupped to ear, leaned forward listening to the young firebrand with the hint of a smile. Behind him the Liberal faithful flung their hats in the air.' Naturally she was pleased that the speech had been a success, but she could not help hoping that her father had not read it. She reflected also that Bernard would be spending Christmas in one of those antiquated and hereditary entrenchments, even though it did not belong to a peer.

Of course she said nothing of such thoughts, but only congratulated him on his success, when he came into her work room. He was looking particularly elegant, in a tweed suit with turned-down collar and striped tie.

'Yes, a little abuse does rouse the populace at times, although one mustn't repeat it too often. I have some news which you should keep to yourself. The old man will be going early in the New Year. He is very deaf, you know, and finds it hard to hear everything that's said. And then I think he has given up hope of seeing an Irish Bill put through in this Parliament.'

'And the new Prime Minister will be Lord Rosebery?'

'It will be Rosebery, and everyone knows Rosebery thinks an Irish Bill is a hopeless proposition, so things will stay as they are.'

'Which means there will be more trouble in Ireland.'

'There will be more trouble in Ireland. But one must face reality. There is no majority for an Irish Bill in the English constituencies, so that it can only be passed with the help of the Irish Members. The House of Lords have thrown it out once, and they will do so again.'

'Until they are driven from their entrenchments by force?'

'You put it very well, but that won't happen tomorrow, or next week. In the meantime there is some other news, also secret. MacMurdo is giving up in the New Year, and I am to be made Under Secretary to Morley.'

He spoke so calmly that for the moment she did not take in the full impact of it. Then she was in his arms, kissing him and saying how proud she was to be his wife. He pooh-poohed her words, saying that it was no more than a single step up a long ladder, but she could tell that he was pleased. Then she felt the arm that she was holding stiffen, and looking at his olive face saw that it was drained of colour. He was staring at her desk, but when she turned to see what was there it contained only such familiar things as forms for her work at Whitechapel, the inkstand with the metal pen she had been using, her ivory-handled paper knife, photographs of her mother and father, Roderick and Nelly, to which had been added recently a photograph of Charlie Bangs standing at an easel, with Nelly beside him and two other figures visible behind them.

'Bernard, what's the matter?'

He moved out of her arms. 'I felt a sudden pain round my heart, but it has gone now. For a moment it made me catch my breath.'

149

She did not believe him. What could possibly have alarmed him in a photograph of Charlie Bangs?

PART TWO

CHRISTMAS AT CHADDERLEY

1 Getting There

Chadderley was near to the village of Elham in Kent, and getting there was by no means simple. The train from London took you as far as Canterbury, or rather to Harbledown Junction just outside the city, where it was necessary to change onto the Elham Valley Light Railway, which ran for little more than sixteen miles to Cheriton, on the outskirts of Folkestone. The carriages were old, the jolting was considerable, and the beauty of the scenery was hidden under a quilt of snow on the day before Christmas Eve when Bernard and Dolly made the journey, accompanied by Lizzie who came nominally as lady's maid, but in truth because Dolly thought she would be miserable if left behind at Kensington. She had never travelled in a train before, and Dolly took care to see that she was safely settled in a second-class compartment before going along to their more comfortable first-class. The second-class carriage was full, but no other passengers disturbed Dolly and Bernard. The contrast struck Dolly.

'Do you suppose, Bernard, that when the peers have been thrown out of their gilded chambers and are no longer in their hereditary entrenchments, there will be no different classes on the railway? Shall we all travel in the same carriages? That might not be altogether comfortable.'

Bernard laid down the *Strand Magazine*, which he had bought at the station bookstall. 'I beg your pardon?' She repeated what she had said. 'Irony does not become you, Dolly.'

'It was a serious question.'

'Very well. While there are masters and men, or ladies and

153

ladies' maids, there will be different classes on our railways.' He turned to the magazine and she to a novel by Henry James called *The Tragic Muse*, which had been recommended to her by Matilda, but which she found rather slow.

They had to wait an hour at Harbledown for their train connection, and the carriages on this branch were unheated. Bernard was ruffled out of his usual good temper, and said that the service was the result of a feud between two companies, and that the Government would have to take some decisive steps to improve the railways. She began to feel nervous about the forthcoming holiday.

'Chadderley is not the kind of place you are used to, Bernard.'

'What do you mean? I have stayed at country houses before.'

She did not remind him that he had done so only once, and that the house had belonged to a very rich Liberal peer. 'That was the kind of place where everything runs as smoothly as a machine. Chadderley is – well, it is not like that. I love it because we used to spend summers there when we were children. There's a kind of lake near the house which we used to swim in, called the Hundred Fathom Pond because it's supposed to be so deep. One of my uncles drowned there, and his body was never found. Then there were picnics, and games in the grounds, and I remember the weather as always sunny, although I suppose that can't have been true. But at this time of year it can be uncomfortable.'

'You talk about the kind of place I am used to. I daresay it will be no colder or more uncomfortable than some of the rooms I lived in when I first came to England.'

'Bernard, I will not be rebuked in that way. You know nothing about English country life, and I was trying to prepare you for it, that is all.'

He smiled, said that he was sorry, and that he was under a lot of pressure in relation to Parliamentary affairs. Then he went back to his magazine.

When they reached Elham station snow was falling. They were the only passengers to leave the train, and the single porter took their bags to the entrance. A snowy waste confronted them.

'Bateman should have sent a carriage to meet us. No doubt it will be here soon.' She did not say that the absence of the carriage was a foretaste of what might be expected at Chadderley.

'It should be here now. How far is the house?'

'I don't know. Perhaps three miles.'

'Then I think we should take a cab. I suppose there is one?'

They consulted the porter, who said that the cab had been taken by somebody off the last train who wanted to go to a house the other side of Rhodes Minnis, so that it wouldn't be back for an hour or so. They retreated to the waiting room where Lizzie, who looked more than usual like a pinched small bird, took off her gloves and tried to warm her hands in front of some of the smouldering coals. It was half an hour before they heard the sound of horses' hooves, and Roderick appeared in the doorway, wearing a large Inverness coat and woollen cap, his face almost invisible behind a huge scarf.

'Sorry to be so bally late. Snow's piled up, thought I might have to dig my way through it. Come on then, here we go.' He lifted a couple of bags and Bernard, an expression of distaste on his face, took others. The porter was nowhere to be seen. Dolly exclaimed when she saw that the carriage was a light victoria.

'Why didn't you bring the brougham?'

155

'Shaft broke a couple of months ago, and Bateman didn't send it for repair. Now, young woman, you travel outside with me, so up you go.' Bernard and Dolly entered the carriage, Roderick jumped up beside Lizzie, and away they went through Elham's pretty little square and out of the village. They went along a narrow lane to Chadderley village, and after that the journey was mostly uphill, but they managed it without having to get out and dig, and rattled up the drive of Chadderley House.

Chadderley had originally been a small eighteenth century manor house, built by an earlier Detling, but it had been added to at various times so that the general impression was Gothic. The original symmetry had been deliberately destroyed by a local architect named Petchey, who had made sure that his additions at the back and side had high pointed roofs which dwarfed the original. There were other bits of roof on different levels, gables, oriel windows and a whole extra wing topped by a tower, which made the structure into the shape of an "L". Much of the interior had been changed to fit in with the alterations. Petchey was delighted with his work, and so was the Detling of the period. Whether or not the architectural irregularities were pleasing, however, there could be no doubt that Chadderley was an awkward house to live in.

From the big entrance courtyard you came into a hall, with the billiard room to one side of it, Sir Arthur's study on the other, and a staircase going up to the bedrooms. At the back of the house were drawing and dining rooms, with a vast conservatory added by Petchey which led out of the drawing room. A morning room had been stuck on one side and the kitchen quarters on the other, so that smells from both directions often seeped into it. Perhaps for this reason, the morning room was little used. The addition forming the short wing of the "L" contained kitchen, scullery, butler's pantry, larders, boot room, bottle store and servants' hall, and a hand operated lift for luggage, to avoid carrying it upstairs. The servants' quarters were thus kept completely separate, as was desirable, but the first floor above them contained guest bedrooms, in which again smells drifted up from below.

Bernard and Dolly found themselves in one of these rooms. They were large, had high ceilings and long narrow windows, so that they were both dark and cold. Petchey had indulged himself with the fireplaces. They were high and arched, with animal heads set into the top of the arch which was steep and narrow, the grate below being correspondingly small. It was late afternoon, and the light had almost gone. Bernard looked for a central chandelier, but did not see it.

'We have no gas,' Dolly said. 'There is no public gasworks near, and father did not think it worth the expense of building our own. But they should have put lamps in the room.'

As she spoke there was a knock at the door, and a procession entered, led by a bowed old man with a white beard. He was followed by three boys bearing oil lamps which they distributed in various positions. The lamps cast a yellow glow over the immediately adjacent areas, which made the rest of the room seem even darker.

'Miss Dolly,' the old man said in a voice that wavered like a plucked violin string. 'I hope I see you well, Miss Dolly.'

'Thank you, Bateman. It is Mrs Ross now. And this is Mr Ross.'

The old man lifted his head with some effort, to reveal a wizened monkey face in part hidden by the beard. 'It is an honour to meet you, sir. I have been with Sir Arthur, and his father too, for nearly fifty years, and have known Miss Dolly and Miss Nelly since they were in their cots. And Mr

157

Roderick, of course. Three bonnier children never drew breath. Of course in those days Chadderley was occupied far, far more than it is nowadays.'

'I hope you are keeping well, Bateman,' Dolly said.

'I mustn't complain, Miss Dolly, what good ever came of complaining? I still have my old trouble, which I fear has got worse. I have difficulty in keeping my head up, sir,' he explained to Bernard. 'It droops, you see, the neck seems not strong enough to hold up the head. But otherwise I am in fair health, although not able to do as much as I did. If Lady Detling had given me more time to make preparations, things might have been more as I would have wished, but that's the way of the world nowadays. If there is anything you require, however, I shall do my best to see that you have it. I am not always able to be sure that things have been done quite as they should, because of this trouble with my head.'

'Thank you, Bateman. If we need anything we shall ring.'

Bateman shuffled to the door. 'I ordered that tea should be served on your arrival, Miss Dolly, and I trust that has been done.'

When the door was closed Bernard said, 'I can see what Roderick meant about the need to pension him off. I should like to wash off some of the journey's grime before going down, and so I expect would you. I suppose –' He stopped, and looked at her. She shook her head.

'There is no running hot water. Father says that what was good enough for grandfather is good enough for him. So of course there is no bathroom. There is a hip bath in the corner, and a wash basin. You are not in London now, you know.'

He burst out laughing, and took her in his arms. 'I shall never need a pin to puncture my self-esteem, shall I, when you are there to do it? Shall we ring for some hot water?'

158

2 A Game of Billiards

'A white Christmas,' Matilda said. 'Don't you consider that perfect? What is it the poet says? "Let the wind whistle as it will, we'll keep our Christmas merry still." And then, "Where the snow lay all about, deep and white and even".'

'Crisp, mamma, not white,' Nelly said. 'And Good King Wenceslas is a carol, not a poem.'

They sat in the drawing room, after a dinner that had not been a great success, because some of the dishes had been burnt, while other were underdone. There was a big grate in the room, and the fire was kept blazing, but a powerful draught swept in from the conservatory. Bernard and Dolly had been the last arrivals, and the party was now complete.

Sir Arthur found himself sitting next to Blader and asked, with not much idea of what he meant by the phrase, 'What are things like in the City, then?'

'Capital, couldn't be better.'

'Glad to hear it. From what I can see, the rest of the country's gone to the devil in a hand-cart. I don't know what they're thinking of in Parliament. They say they call Gladstone G.O.M. for Grand Old Man, but I call him Grand Old Muddler. Parliament sitting until five days before Christmas, I never heard anything like it.'

Blader's round weighty face glowed with enthusiasm. 'I'll tell you what I believe in, and it's something I learned at my father's knee. I believe in co-operation. If we all work together to keep the wheels turning, if we remember that trade and business enterprise are our life blood, then the country will flourish. When the stock market's healthy, there can't be much

159

wrong with Britain is what I say. And that reminds me. Take one of these, Sir Arthur. You too, Roderick. Charlie, Bernard. Just four of them left.'

Sir Arthur looked at the cylinder with distaste. 'What the devil is it?'

'A new invention, British as the Union Jack, which I'm proud to say I'm going to market. And I owe a debt of gratitude to young Roderick here for bringing it to my attention. This is a fountain pen containing an amazing substance that will very likely replace ink, and it will last for a year or more without refilling.'

'Fountain pens. Never use 'em.' Sir Arthur's noble head was raised in an expression of disdain, and indeed the production of the pens and the way in which Blader spoke of them smacked uncommonly of a salesman's patter.

'Just try it, that's all I ask.'

'Ha. Very well.' Sir Arthur tucked away the pen. Bella had been sitting placidly in an armchair, apparently on the verge of sleep, but now she was moved to speech.

'Joe talks of nothing except these pens and an American gentleman, Mr Hatherley, who's made some wonderful investments, so Joe says.'

'Is that Mr Duncan Hatherley?' Dolly asked. 'The gentleman you brought round one day, Roderick, when we were out.'

Roderick said that was the same Mr Hatherley, and Gertrude announced that he was one of the most perfect gentlemen she had ever met.

'A great investor,' Blader said. 'A man who makes up his mind without wasting your time or his. I want this, I'll have that, he says, and settles on the nail. I don't suppose you'll have heard of him, Bernard, seeing that you were in the Midwest, but he's known as Lucky Hatherley in New York. I can tell you I took to him as a man, quite apart from admiring him as an investor.'

At some time during the course of this conversation Paul had appeared. He was so unobtrusive that his presence or absence in a room was hardly noticeable. Sir Arthur got up, and said that he was going to work in his study. He felt that he could stay no longer in the same room with Blader. 'Settles on the nail', indeed. It was the kind of talk you might expect to hear from a grocer or a tailor. To think that his son was married to the daughter of such a man.

Matilda protested that she had wanted her husband to join in playing a Christmas game, but he said that it was not yet even Christmas Eve, and stumped off. When he had gone they went on talking. A game of charades was proposed, but Dolly said she thought they should keep those until Christmas Day. Instead, the gentlemen stood round the piano and accompanied Matilda, as she played old songs. Roderick, who had a strong baritone voice, sang *Oh No, We Never Mention Her* with a hand on his heart:

> *Oh, no! we never mention her, her name is never heard;*
> *My lips are now forbid to speak that once familiar word:*
> *From sport to sport they hurry me, to banish my regret;*
> *And when they win a smile from me, they think that I forget.*

Then Nelly and Charlie Bangs sang *Home, Sweet Home* as a duet, and they all went on to *Little Boy Blue, The Mistletoe Bough,* and a number of others, ending up with Mrs Norton's stirring *The Arab's Farewell to His Steed.* It was the kind of evening Matilda very much enjoyed, and by the end of it most of them were feeling that curious cheerfulness caused by singing together, which has almost the effect of an intoxicant.

Dolly had noticed that Bernard was an exception. He took part in one or two of the songs, but his attention seemed elsewhere. When Paul Patterwick asked if he would care for a game of billiards he accepted very readily, which meant that she had to go up to bed alone. Of course, this was something she had done often enough before at Chadderley, but she was a little annoyed that he should not come up with her on the first night of their stay.

The colza oil lamps set over the billiard table created patches of bright light on the green baize which alternated with bands of semi darkness. The two men had hardly spoken a dozen words to each other when being introduced. Now, after they had each played a couple of strokes, Paul said, 'I work in the Home Office. In the Irish section.'

Bernard had lighted one of his Abdullas. He played a couple of cannons, then missed an easy pot on the red. 'I fear I'm a little rusty.'

'My work is to keep files on any terrorist or suspected terrorist in Britain and the United States. I expect you know something about it.'

'I know that the section exists, of course, but the details are not revealed to minor Parliamentarians.' He bent over the table again, played a delicate shot to put his own ball into the pocket off the red, and went on to make a break of thirty. Paul regarded himself as a very fair player, but saw to his surprise that Bernard was a better one.

'I work closely with Inspector Moss of the Yard, who has particular responsibility for Irish matters as far as they concern the police.'

'Ah yes. One of the estimable British bulldogs.'

'He tells me that he came to see you about the death of Settleby.' Bernard said nothing. 'And about your connection with Devas and his friends.'

Bernard took a step forward, cue in hand, and Paul retreated slightly, only to find that the other merely wanted to chalk his cue. Then Bernard leaned on his cue, and spoke with a trace of amusement. 'Mr Patterwick, I thought we came here to play billiards, but it seems you want to ask me some questions about Ireland. If that is your intention, I must say that this is not the time or place for it.'

'I know that.' Paul looked more like a nervous mouse than usual. 'But I wanted you to understand my concern. There is something very wrong about what is happening lately. Things have not been as they should, and I am afraid of some awful event, an attack on a member of the Royal family or something of the kind. I thought you would feel as I do.'

'If I shared your fears, no doubt I should.'

'I wanted to ask you about that remarkable statement you made that Devas tried to bribe you to give him information.'

'So the British bulldog told you that. Perhaps he also told you that I did not take it seriously.'

'It does not sound like a joke. I should have thought that you would have reported it to the police.'

'What an admirable custodian of public morality you are, Mr Patterwick,' Bernard said sarcastically. 'Perhaps you should have been appointed to such a post, instead of as a filing clerk passing on information that seems always to be a few hours or days too late.'

There was a silence in the room, except for the slight hissing of the colza lamps. Paul moved away to the other side of the table.

163

'The information I gather is passed to Scotland Yard. And to Mr MacMurdo. You say he does not inform you about Irish matters, but I have heard that he thinks highly of you.'

'Thank you. I am glad that good news is so widespread.'

'So that he might have told you of the attempt to blow up the Stock Exchange, and the planting of a bomb in Madame Tussaud's.'

'He might have done. But he did not.'

'You know that Scotland Yard never caught any of the people responsible?' Bernard nodded. 'You are known for your sympathy towards Irish Home Rule.'

'So are many M.P.s.'

There were beads of sweat on Paul's forehead, but he went doggedly on. 'The others don't invite Irish terrorists to sit down at table with them. Do you really mean to say that you had no knowledge of these men when you were a young man in the United States?'

Bernard swept his cue round the table, knocking the balls up to the baulk end. 'The game is over, and the questioning with it.'

'You won't say anything further?'

'What more is there to say? I know nothing that will help you, but I can see that you do not believe it.'

'Then I will give *you* a little information that may interest you. A cable has been sent to one of our agents in the Midwest asking for details of your background. But I am sure that there will be nothing to worry you in that.'

Bernard paused at the door. For a moment he seemed about to say something. Then he went out, and closed the door behind him.

3 *Christmas Eve*

Breakfast at Chadderley, like other meals, was announced by a great bronze gong which Bateman struck in the entrance hall at exactly nine o'clock. After beating the gong he pottered along to the dining room and stood between the door and the sideboard with its chafing dishes, his head drooping, ready to greet all comers and to add a warning note to his greeting if they were late. Without actually saying so, he gave the impression of knowing his presence to be indispensable.

Matilda was always early, and on this morning her husband was only a couple of minutes later. The Bladers came down together, just behind him. Sir Arthur's temper had not improved overnight. He lifted the covers of each dish, making a grumbling sound in his throat as he did so, and took a couple of bacon rashers and a sausage.

'Don't get the breakfasts we had when I was a young man,' he said. 'My father would eat a piece of good rump steak or a couple of chops every morning. Don't know what's happened to all that, if you put it on the table nobody would touch it.'

Blader helped himself to poached eggs, sat down and looked at his watch. 'If I were in London I should have been at my desk just ten minutes ago. My motto is do as you would be done by. I'm punctual myself, and I expect punctuality of others.'

'Joe never has more than two slices of toast at breakfast, and a cup of tea. Never varies.'

Sir Arthur fixed Blader with a look of acute dislike, and said 'Ha.'

'I enjoyed our little sing-song last night so much,' Matilda said dreamily. 'The simple old songs, I sometimes think they are the best when all is said. It was a pity you missed it, my dear. But tonight we shall play charades, and I shan't allow you to run away. All the world's a stage, I think that's very true.'

'And all the men and women merely players.' Bernard was one of those men who manage to look particularly fresh and well in the morning. 'I'm sure we shall be happy to act away like anything. I look forward to giving a lifelike representation of a Member of Parliament.'

Upstairs, Dolly was asking her lady's maid what she should wear. She eventually settled on a brown jacket and skirt, which would at least be warm. 'What do you think of Chadderley, Lizzie?'

'It ain't half big, madam. And cold.'

'Yes it is cold. You are not to say "ain't", Lizzie, and especially not to say "it ain't half", this or that.'

'I heard Flora saying "ain't", but I won't if you don't like it. But it is big. And there's nothing here, is there?'

'What do you mean?'

'Out there.' Lizzie gestured towards the window, and the snow. 'Nothing out there, is there, madam? No houses and no people, just nothing. I never seen anything like it, it don't seem right to me.'

'In the summer there is green grass and beautiful flowers,' Dolly said sententiously. 'I'm not sure that this brown suits me. What do you think?'

'You look lovely, madam,' Lizzie said fervently.

Nelly had been as good as her word. Her bedroom was next to Charlie's, an arrangement which Matilda had permitted, because at the time she was dealing with some complaint of the cook's relating to Bateman and with the stuffing for the goose.

Nelly had simply said that the green room she had been given was too cold, and she was going to change. Charlie had spent the night in her room, not leaving until five in the morning. She came down to breakfast looking radiant. Charlie, who had fallen asleep as soon as he got back to his own room, apologised profusely for his lateness. Dolly gave him a keen glance, and then looked speculatively at her sister. Paul appeared just after Charlie, looking more than ever like a large white mouse, and Roderick and Gertrude came down together. Billy, of course, was in the care of his nurse.

'I think this snow's here to stay,' Roderick said, staring out of the window after finishing his breakfast. 'What do you say, Bateman? I remember you used to feel rain coming because you had pains in your left leg. The wooden one, you used to say. And we jolly well believed you had a wooden leg, you know.'

Bateman's head rose cautiously as a tortoise's emerging from its shell, and his shoulders trembled a little, so that he might have been understood to be laughing. 'I remember very well, Mr Roderick.'

'So what's your left leg telling you now? Don't want to be cooped up here all day like bally chickens. Thought Paul and I might take a couple of the gee gees out, ride over to see the Rainbirds at Barham.'

'You'll do nothing of the kind,' his father said. 'With the roads as they are the horses would be floundering in five minutes. Might break a leg. I absolutely forbid it.'

'My left leg aches something terrible, Mr Roderick. It's either more snow, or else it's rain. Is it your wish that I should go about my household duties now, my lady?'

'What's that? Oh yes, Bateman, by all means. And make sure the fires are kept up, won't you?' When he had gone Matilda sighed. 'Poor Bateman, he's in the sere and yellow

167

leaf, I'm afraid. We should be distributing little gifts in Chadderley village today. I feel there's a duty on one to do it, but if you think the horses shouldn't be taken out –'

'Didn't say that at all,' Sir Arthur said. 'If you get out the victoria and go down to the village, that's one thing. Riding over the fields to Barham is quite another.'

Roderick had been sulking, but his spirits were revived by the prospect of getting out. 'I'll drive you down. Make something to do, won't it? Nothing to do, a fellow gets bally bored. When we get back let's have a billiards tournament, a fiver from everybody in the kitty, winner scoops the pool. Feel like coming down to the village, Paul? Oh very well, what about you, Bernard?'

'I have some letters to write.'

'In any case I should like one or both of the girls to come with me,' Matilda said.

Her son laughed. 'Just what I thought you'd say, mamma. When we get stuck in a drift, will you and the girls want to dirty your dresses? Oh well, I suppose some kitchen lad can come along – unless you'd care to, old man?' This was said to Charlie, who expressed himself happy to go along with the party.

Before they left, Dolly said to her sister, 'Are you intending to announce your engagement? If not, I think you should be more circumspect in your behaviour.'

'Oh, fudge,' Nelly replied. 'Really, Dolly, you are like an old maid sometimes. Of course we're not going to announce our engagement, that kind of thing is quite out-of-date.'

'Then you shouldn't look at that young man as if you were a moon-struck heifer.' She added tartly, 'And so far from being being an old maid, I would remind you that I have been married only six months.'

'Nobody would know. For goodness sake stop *fussing*.'

168

Nelly disappeared into her bedroom, and Dolly looked after her thoughtfully. It had not escaped her notice that her room was next to that occupied by Charlie Bangs.

Day or night, rain or shine, the "shadower" must follow his quarry's every movement. The detective knows that at any moment the man followed may realise himself pursued, and turn on the pursuer with a knife or revolver. Nominally, you are on shadowing duty only for a certain time, but there's the rub. You may begin in Shepherd's Bush and find yourself obliged to follow your man to the Mile End Road; you may telegraph the Yard for your relief to meet you somewhere in Euston Road, but before he can get there you may have had to hurry off to Finsbury. The good shadower must have perseverance, presence of mind, and resourcefulness, and he must know London well so that he does not let himself be decoyed into some cul-de-sac where he is quietly disposed of.

So Moss wrote in his memoirs some years later, to emphasise that shadowing was not easy work. However, in pursuit of his view that a detective was most usefully occupied out in the streets, he had spent the previous day shadowing Devas and his friends. His companions had been Sergeant Blakey, and two detective constables named Stewart and Shires. In spite of the bold words written in his memoirs, Moss was in no doubt that his quarries knew him by sight, even if they did not recognise the constables. They shadowed in couples, in spells of three hours at a time, and it worked well enough, except when the Irishmen took cabs.

They spent an hour in the British Museum, and then two more at the Museum Tavern nearby, where they got talking with some of the attendants, and stood them several rounds of drinks. Then on to Madam Tussaud's and another session of drinking, then to the Alhambra where they met a couple of soldiers they had been seen with a few days earlier down at Woolwich. At least Blakey and Stewart thought they were two of the same group, although they could not be sure. Moss himself had not been doing any shadowing on that day. All this involved some drinking by the policemen, and Moss had not been pleased after the Museum Tavern session to find Shires glassy-eyed and with slightly slurred speech.

'Hold up, man, you're falling about all over the place. What would you do if a couple of those Irish villains got you down an alley?'

'They'd feel the weight of this, sir' The constable slowly and blunderingly produced a truncheon.

'They'd have your guts for garters before you had a chance to use it. You've got to learn how to make half a pint last an hour, Shires. As for you, Sergeant Blakey, you should have known better than let a man get into this condition. You'd better get off home, Shires, you're useless for any kind of work. I'll have a word to say to you tomorrow.'

When the sergeant asked whether he should get a replacement, Moss said that he would do the duty himself. The rebukes were fully justified, but in practice it was difficult not to down a few glasses of beer as the hours went by. It was not as though the Irishmen settled anywhere, so that a man could go off and get a bite to eat. If they were in a pub, one or the other of them was slipping away to the gents, or going to play a game of darts or dominoes while the two others propped up the bar. At the Alhambra it looked for a while as though they and the soldiers might become involved with some of the prostitutes flaunting themselves about, but in the end they went no further than conversation. When the music hall closed the five men went down to Charing Cross station, where among a good deal of back-slapping the soldiers caught their train to Woolwich. Duty was not finished even then, for the Irishmen

170

visited another pub before taking a cab back to their Clerkenwell lodgings. By the time Moss got back to his home in
Kennington, where his wife greeted him with the news that he
had been drinking, he was beginning to think that their activity
was just a waste of time.

The following day had to be spent at the Yard, with a
different group of plain clothes men doing the shadowing. The
Inspector's head ached, and he was in no mood to deal with the
pile of paper and reports that lay on his desk, most of them
relating to Settleby. The painter had been much disliked for
his rudeness, but he had no particular enemies, and although
there were plenty of people to say that he had often been flush
with money recently, none of them knew where it had come
from. Moss closed his eyes. He had had no more than four
hours' sleep.

He opened his eyes again when one of the clerks came in
with a cable, and by the time he had read it he was wide awake.
The message was from the Irish section's man in Chicago. It
said that he could find no trace of a family named Ross who
had lived in the Gardville Grove area, nor was a man with that
name known to have had a fancy goods business in Chicago.
The cable asked for more details so that enquiries could be
continued. Why should Ross have lied about his background?
The suspicion that he was a member of the Irish Republican
Brotherhood who had managed to get into Britain's Parliament was revived in the Inspector's mind. He busied himself
during the rest of the morning in gathering together what information he could find about Ross, and sent off another cable.

After that, much of the day was spent in what he sometimes
called wastepaper basket work, filling in forms, and attending
meetings which were not connected with Irish affairs, but his
thoughts were with Devas and his friends. It was nearly five in
the afternoon when he was called to take a telephone call from

Blakey. There were telephones at the Yard, but none in or near the Inspector's office, since in general the telegraph office was regarded as a safer means of communication. Moss was called into the office of the Chief Constable, who ranked next to the Assistant Commissioner in the CID hierarchy. The Chief Constable indicated displeasure.

'One of your men has called up, Moss. He is *there*.' He pointed to the instrument. 'This kind of thing is a confounded nuisance. I hope the fellow has a good reason for using the machine.'

Moss picked up the receiver. 'Detective Inspector Moss speaking.' An unintelligible bellow came down the line. 'No need to shout, man, I'm not deaf. Take it quietly, tell me why you're telephoning. Begin with name and rank.'

'Yes, sir. Sarn't Blakey speaking.' There was silence.

'Well? Go on.'

'In Clerkenwell Green Post Office, sir. It seemed convenient to use the telephone, the matter being possibly urgent. If it was an error, sir, I can only say –'

'Never mind, Blakey. Say what you've got to say.'

'Yes sir. Concerning Mr Devas and friends, I have to report that they have been watched throughout the day. They did not leave their Clerkenwell lodgings until approximately two fifteen pip emma, when they took the omnibus to Charing Cross. There they met off the Woolwich train the two soldiers seen on the previous evening as you, sir, are aware. The party repaired to the *Welsh Harp* nearby, and consumed –'

With the Chief Constable glaring at him across the room, Moss felt fury rising. 'Sergeant, tell me your reason for making this call. Immediately, do you understand?'

He heard a deep breath being drawn. Then there was speech. 'Some of 'em are still here, Inspector, and one gone off, and I thought we should stay keeping watch on the lodgings, you said don't split up without informing you, but they've been inside for a couple of hours now, and I dunno if I've done right.'

'Sergeant,' Moss shouted. 'Are you telling me that the three Irishmen went into their lodging house, and then one came out more than two hours back? And that you didn't follow him?'

'S'right, sir. See Shires isn't the brightest, and I thought I should stay here.'

'Which one was it? Was he alone?'

'Which one, sir, I couldn't rightly say. He wasn't alone, he was with the two soldiers. They came out of the pub half seas over, and then went into the house, the whole lot of them. After half an hour or a little less they came out, and they were walking straight as a ruler, all three. Sobered up, I suppose.'

'Blakey, get into that lodging house. Don't take no for an answer, you must see the Irishmen. Take Shires with you. I'll tell you what I think you'll find.'

He told Blakey, then hung up the telephone. 'I hope the use of that instrument justified the inconvenience caused,' the Chief Constable said.

'I think so, sir. If you will excuse me I must leave for Woolwich at once. I hope I shall be in time.'

'What for?'

'Unless I'm much mistaken, sir, they plan to blow up part of the Woolwich Barracks.'

Mr Duncan J. Hatherley dressed with his usual care that morning, and packed his bags with the feeling of pleasure induced when everything has gone as smoothly as could be wished. England had made him welcome but it was time to leave, for France and then perhaps Germany. He had heard that the French loved a gambler, a man ready to spend money. He rang for his bags to be taken down, and asked that a cab should be called to take him to Victoria. As he brushed a perhaps imaginary fleck of dust from his jacket, he felt a touch of regret. There was an incompleteness about this visit to England, a respect in which his intentions had not been fulfilled.

He thought about it, and said aloud, 'Why not?' Chadderley was, after all, only a few miles from Dover, and although it might be out of the way, what did that matter? He could cross the Channel on Christmas morning rather than on the night of Christmas Eve if need be. It meant taking a chance perhaps, but when had he ever refused to take a chance? Besides, it would be pleasant to see Blader again, and to smoke one of his cigars. At Victoria he made enquiries about how he could reach Chadderley in Kent, and found himself on the train to Canterbury. The prospect ahead continued to amuse him during the journey.

Bernard had brought down a box of papers to read, and another containing letters to be answered, and since there was no library at Chadderley he used the morning room. Smells floated in from the kitchen quarters, and there was a miserable fire, but he ignored both odours and discomfort, and settled down to letter writing, using Blader's pen. It certainly wrote with wonderful smoothness, and without the occasional blotchiness of the ordinary fountain pen. He did not hear the door open behind him, but turned when a delicate cough announced another presence. It was Paul Patterwick.

'Excuse me. I hope I won't disturb you if I use the desk over there in the corner.'

'Not at all.'

Patterwick's lashes fluttered. He was very nervous. 'I feel I must apologise for the way in which I spoke last night. Some of my questions were – I should not have asked them. I can only

174

say I was overwrought. I slept little, and thought about what had been said in relation to Settleby, and other matters. I think I understand a little more now. I hope you will forgive me for what may have seemed an impertinence.'

'You are forgiven,' Bernard said, and returned to his letters. He had his back to Patterwick, but heard the scratch of the other's pen. When he had finished his letters and got up to leave, Patterwick was still at the desk, but no longer writing. With pen beside him, he sat staring at the wall.

The trip to Chadderley village turned out to be a success. Matilda had provided herself with a number of small presents, and moved naturally into the part of Lady Bountiful. The young men acted as porters, with Roderick making bad jokes, and Dolly and Nelly, who had not seen most of the villagers for years, patted babies on the head and agreed that time flew by, and that it was nice to see a white Christmas. Dolly asked questions about the cost of things, especially food, until her sister told her that they might be resented at Christmas.

'Isn't mamma splendid?' Nelly said to Charlie. 'You'd never guess that she doesn't know half their names.'

'She is full of elan vital, the life force. Do you think she would let me sketch her?'

'Not if you make one of those gloomy drawings of yours, showing her as Medusa or a harpy. You have a very nasty imagination, Mr Bangs. Give me your arm, it's slippery.'

Driving back was not quite so easy as going down, but they managed it without trouble. Roderick offered to wager a fiver that he could get back in less than fifteen minutes, but Charlie refused, saying that Roderick would simply land them in a ditch. Even without a bet, Roderick drove with great dash, and they all looked pinkly healthy when they got out, stamping their feet in the entrance. At luncheon Matilda expanded on

175

the pleasures of country life.

'When I saw those honest faces in the village today, so friendly and so pleased to see me, I felt how artificial is the life we all lead in town. "I too lived in Arcadia", how true that is.'

'Mamma, you know you don't think it's true at all,' Dolly said impatiently. 'You'd be tired of life down here in three months. And as for being happy to see us, you'd have heard a different tale as soon as our backs were turned. You should be with me in the East End. There they say rude things to our faces.'

'East London is one thing, Dolly, Chadderley quite another,' her mother said serenely. 'They are simple country folk down here. So many of them spoke of you, Sir Arthur, and said how pleased they were that the family is in residence for Christmas.'

Blader shook his head. 'At the same time, Lady Detling, the business of the world goes on in cities. Your good country folk would be poor as church mice if it weren't for commerce.'

'Joe always says that,' Bella remarked proudly. Dolly's remark that most of the country folk *were* as poor as church mice was, fortunately perhaps, lost in the buzz of conversation.

After lunch the spirit of jollity was maintained, as Roderick organised the billiards tournament, which included ladies as well as gentlemen. Paul retired to his room with a headache, and Matilda said that she must make sure all the preparations for the evening were in train, but the rest of them had a lively time. Roderick put all the names in a hat, and they were drawn out to decide the matches. Then, using the Everlasting Pen, he wrote out the names and handicaps, and pinned up the sheet beside the scoring board. The ladies were given an eighty start in a hundred, and the men were handicapped according to the form they showed.

Sir Arthur joined in and, to everybody's surprise except his own, played some brilliant screw shots and got into the final, where he was beaten by Dolly. The games were played to the accompaniment of much laughter, some of it prompted by Bateman, who insisted on keeping the score, and had to be corrected frequently because his drooping head meant that he failed to notice a number of scoring strokes. Gertrude was beaten in the first round, and said that she must look after Billy, who was teething, but the other players stayed on as audience, drifting in and out of the billiard room, and giving vociferous cheers for good or lucky shots. Afterwards Bateman quaveringly recalled the past.

'It took me back, sir, took me back many years. I recall in your father's day, how the two of you would be at the table, playing the whole morning sometimes. He was a fine player, your father.'

'Ha,' Sir Arthur said, but he was not displeased. 'Something you never lose once you've learned it, how to tickle the ivories. Though billiards is like everything else, going to rack and ruin. They're using these composition balls now, so I hear, even at Thurston's. Haven't got the feel of the ivories, won't have them in the house, and won't use 'em in the Club. You've learned how to make a bridge,' he said to Dolly. 'Not many women can do it.'

'I don't think much skill is involved in using a stick to knock three balls around a table.' Dolly saw her husband's frown, and added meekly, 'But thank you.'

Then it was tea time, curtains drawn, scones and biscuits, bread and butter and jam, sandwiches, and a Christmas cake, all served in the drawing room. The first cups were being poured when a maid brought in a card to Matilda, who looked at it through a lorgnette.

Mr Duncan J. Hatherley. I don't think the name is known to me.'

There were exclamations of pleasure from Roderick, Gertrude and her father, and Mr Hatherley's identity was explained. A couple of minutes later the man himself was in the room. He bowed over Matilda's hand.

'Lady Detling, I must apologise for calling like this, unannounced on Christmas Eve. The truth is that I have been called unexpectedly to the Continent on business, and didn't want to leave without saying goodbye to my friend Mr Blader. I knew that he was staying here, along with your son and your charming daughter-in-law, whom I've also had the pleasure of meeting. And since this is almost on my way to Dover –' A flashing smile completed the explanation.

Matilda was gracious and Sir Arthur, still warmed by the pleasure of billiards, was genial. The American was introduced by Roderick, and had a few words for everybody. When they came to Dolly and Bernard, who sat together on a sofa, Roderick said, 'My sister, Dolly. You remember that we called but had no luck, they were out.'

Hatherley smiled. 'Immediately recognisable as the daughter of your beautiful mother, if I may say so.'

'And my brother-in-law Bernard Ross, a fellow countryman of yours.'

'Mr Ross, delighted to meet you.' Fingers touched. 'What part of the States are you from?'

'Near Chicago. But I have lived in England for some years.'

'And I hear from Roderick that you are a Member of Parliament, the first I have met. Now, when I get back, I shall be able to tell them that I have shaken hands with somebody who has taken his place in the mother of Parliaments. Believe it or not, a lot of us still think of it that way. And I'll be able to tell them what a British M.P. looks like, one who's American-born, that is.'

'My husband was born here, Mr Hatherley,' Dolly said. 'His

family emigrated to your country when he was a baby.'

'Is that so, now? Very interesting,' Hatherley said with an agreeable smile. Dolly felt a kind of click in her mind, as though there was some kind of reference that she should remember. Then Gertrude asked archly whether Mr Hatherley could tell them what he would be doing on the Continent or whether it was a business secret, and the moment was lost.

'Why, Mrs Detling, I shall mix business with pleasure as I always do. They say that French food is the best in the world, and French women the most beautiful. I find the first easier to believe than the second, now that I have been in England, but I mean to test both propositions.' The colour naturally in Gertrude's cheeks was heightened. 'And I shall hope to do some business, in France and elsewhere, and to find somebody who will be my counsellor and friend, as Mr Blader has been here.'

Blader laughed heartily, and said the pleasure had been mutual. The question arose of whether it would not be easier and more comfortable for Mr Hatherley to stay the night, but it proved that he had arranged for the cab from Elham station to pick him up, and he had already discovered the time of a connection for Dover. Within a few minutes the cab had arrived and the American, still smiling, had said his goodbyes.

A small chorus of praise followed his departure, ranging from Matilda who said that he seemed a wonderfully cultivated man, through Gertrude who praised his beautiful manners, to Blader who said that you couldn't meet an easier man to deal with in the way of business.

In the railway carriage to Dover, Hatherley settled back with a sigh of satisfaction, pleased that he had not denied himself that last touch of reminiscence.

'Madam.' It was Lizzie. 'Can I say something?'

Dolly had been dozing in one of the bedroom armchairs. 'You must knock before coming into a room, Lizzie.' 'I did, but you never answered. So I came in.' What was to be done with such a girl? She held back the sharp words on her tongue. 'What is it?'

'Madam, I think I'm going to have a baby.'

If Dolly had been still half asleep, she was so no longer. She sat upright. '*Lizzie*. What have you been doing?'

Lizzie stood in front of her, a woebegone small bird. 'I done nothing. I been interfered with.'

'Here, do you mean? In this house?' The girl nodded. 'Who was it, Lizzie? You must tell me now, you must say who did this awful thing.'

She said in a low voice, 'It was the old man.'

What would be an old man to Lizzie? 'Do you mean Mr Blader?' Lizzie shook her head. What other old man was there? Dolly thought of her father, and a shiver ran down her spine. She was trying to find a form of words, when Lizzie spoke again.

'The *old* man, I mean. Walks about with 'is head down.'

'You mean *Bateman*?' Lizzie nodded. Dolly suppressed an inclination to laugh. Was it possible that Bateman . . ? She asked the girl to tell her about it.

'My mum said you must never let a man interfere with you, and if you did you had a baby. That's what the old man did, he interfered with me.'

'What exactly happened, Lizzie?'

''E come up behind me and touched me 'ere. Then he lifted up me skirt and put his hand 'ere.'

'Is that all?'

The girl looked astonished. 'Ain't it enough?'

'It was very wrong, but it isn't enough to give you a baby.' Dolly was practical, and disapproved of ignorance. She told

Lizzie just what had to happen before she had a baby. Lizzie was astonished.

'Well, I never. You mean you got to go through all that before you get a baby? I seen those things on my brothers, but I never knew what they was for.'

'Now you know. If you find Bateman doing anything like that again, tell him if he doesn't stop at once you will speak to me.'

At Woolwich Barracks Moss found it hard to reach anybody in authority, and met with scepticism when he eventually spoke to the Adjutant, who had been called away from a Christmas party. After listening to Moss for five minutes, however, the Adjutant gave the Scotland Yard man *carte blanche* to investigate.

Celebrations were in full swing in and around the barracks, but the guard at the gate remembered a couple of gunners who had come back around five thirty, had retained their passes because they said they had only returned to barracks for a few minutes, and then duly left for an evening on the town before six o'clock. Their names were Jones and Gadney. Had he looked at them particularly? Why no, the guard said, why would he do that when it was Christmas Eve and he didn't know either man from Adam? It took a little while to find the number of their barrack room, and a few more minutes to get it cleared ready for a search. They found one small portmanteau among the personal belongings stowed at the end of Gadney's bed, and another over in the dining hall beneath a chair. They were the usual type, tubes of nitro-glycerine with clockwork attachments of American origin, both timed to go off at seven thirty that evening.

'That'd be just when the lads were sitting down to dinner or on the way over from the barrack rooms, so that it would cause the most casualties,' Moss said to his wife Clara that night. 'When Blakey told me the Irishmen had split up, one going off with the soldiers, I knew something was up. It was the first time they'd separated completely, those three, and common-sense said there must be a reason for it. They'd doped the two soldier lads, stripped 'em and taken their uniforms. Then they went down to Woolwich with Devas, planted their bombs and were away again, leaving a nice Christmas present for John Bull. All the rest was flummery, going to the Tower and the British Museum, standing treat to the Beefeaters and all. They thought if they did enough of that, I'd be put off the scent. But they have to get up early in the morning to fool Sam Moss.'

'And don't I know it.' His wife was his most faithful admirer. 'It's Christmas Day tomorrow, remember. You'll be able to come to Albert's, won't you?'

They had arranged to spend Christmas Day with her brother Albert and his family. The family was large and noisy, and Moss was not sorry to have a chance to back out of the arrangement. He shook his head, looking more melancholy bloodhound than bulldog.

'You're a detective twenty-four hours a day, my dear. There's a matter relating to a certain Member of Parliament where I've got questions that need answering. You may have to go over to Albert on your own. Needs must, I'm afraid, no help for it.'

'Your mother has agreed to let me sketch her,' said Charlie. 'I'm delighted. She has such an interesting head.'

'I shouldn't have thought she could spare time to sit for you.'

'That won't be necessary. I shall just wander about putting glimpses of her down on a pad when she's not aware of it, and then work them up.'

'Charlie.' They were sitting beyond the drawing room in the

conservatory. The place was full of exotic trees and shrubs, and they sat behind a potted palm. 'Something's going on.'

'I don't know what you mean.'

'Didn't you notice the way Bernard looked when Mr Hatherley came in, as though he'd seen a ghost? You were busy with mamma's elan vital, I suppose. And then after tea, Bernard asked me the oddest question, about that lovely evening at the Anarchist Club.' She told him what the question was. 'Don't you think it was a strange question to ask?'

'I suppose so.' He did not seem much interested. He traced a line with his finger from Nelly's forehead, down her nose to her chin. 'You have a beautiful profile.'

'Not equal to mamma's, I expect. I'll tell you something else. Dolly suspects. About us, I mean. She asked this morning whether we were going to announce our engagement. She's an old fusspot.'

'Your sister is a sensible woman.'

'You mean that I am not?'

'You are adorable. But perhaps she is right and we should be more careful. Tonight, I mean.'

'Charlie Bangs, you aren't what I would call an ardent wooer.'

'Anyway, it's time to dress for dinner.'

Upstairs, in the sepulchral gloom of their bedroom, Dolly told her husband about Lizzie and Bateman. He laughed, but as she thought rather half-heartedly.

'What's the matter, Bernard? Is it that man Hatherley? Do you know him?'

'Why do you ask?'

'You are good at controlling your feelings, but when you saw him, just for a moment you seemed horrified.'

'Damn this place. It's so dark one can't see to put in a collar stud. Yes, I know him. Or rather, I used to know him.'

'Does he have some hold over you? Were you mixed up in something with him?'

'He has no hold over me. He belongs to the past, and I told you that for me the past no longer exists. I am not going to revive it.'

She asked more questions, but got nothing further out of him. He went into his dressing room to struggle with his bow tie.

Roderick's and Gertrude's bedroom was in the main part of the house, and so better lighted and less dismal. Nevertheless Gertrude complained.

'This is the most uncomfortable house I have ever been in, Roderick. And so old-fashioned. Surely you could persuade your father at least to install gas lighting? And why not central heating? Daddy told me that he has been to several grand old houses where central heating made every room beautifully warm.'

'He's lucky,' her husband said glumly. They had sent for hot water, and he was washing.

'And the servants are a disgrace. Bateman does not exercise authority in the way he should do.'

'Most of them are from the village, and there are some who won't be needed after we leave. You can't expect them to be like family retainers.'

'Is Bateman a good example of a family retainer?'

Roderick sighed. He knew that it was not possible for him to get the better of an argument with Gertrude.

It was not until they had gathered for a glass of sherry that Paul's absence was noticed. It was remembered that he had retired to his room with a headache, and Matilda asked Bateman to send somebody up to see if he was unwell. Bateman himself returned after five minutes, to say that Mr Patterwick was not in his room.

184

'Not in his room,' Matilda repeated incredulously. 'Then where can he be?' She looked round as though expecting to find him hiding behind the furniture.

Bateman raised his head. 'If I may say so, my lady, I think it possible that Mr Patterwick is lost.'

'*Lost*,' Matilda echoed again, on the same note. 'How can he be lost?'

'Possibly on the way back from the viilage, my lady. I think he had the intention of walking there.'

'Why on earth should he do that?' Roderick asked.

Bateman's head had sunk again. He raised it halfway. 'Mr Patterwick asked me whether there was a Post Office in the village, and I told him that there was. He then asked the distance.'

'You didn't see him set off?'

Bateman shook his lowered head. Asked at what time this conversation had taken place, he could only say that it was shortly after lunch. It proved that he had said also that it was possible to take a short cut to the village across the fields. The other servants were questioned, but none of them had spoken to Paul. Roderick and Bernard looked at his room. Clothes were hanging in the wardrobe, and his bed was undisturbed. His overcoat, however, was missing.

Opinions about what should be done varied, from that of Sir Arthur who was in favour of doing nothing at all, on the ground that nobody could come to harm in walking to Chadderley village, to Roderick who was keen to organise a search party at once. Bernard asked the distance to the village.

'Just over a mile and a half by road, a mile if you cut across the fields, but hang it all, nobody in his senses would do that with the snow still quite thick. Nobody but an old fool like Bateman would ever mention it. It's deuced queer, but one thing's certain. Somehow old Paul's got lost, and we ought to look for him.'

Nobody was inclined to take up this last suggestion, but a search party was organised, consisting of Roderick, Bernard, Charlie, and half-a-dozen servants. No more snow had fallen, and a slight thaw had set in. With blazing torches they explored the grounds, going past the Hundred Fathom Pond, right along the drive, and a little way down the road to the village. After a little more than an hour they gave up. The three young men walked back together. As they came up the drive, Roderick exclaimed, 'You don't suppose he could have fallen into the Hundred Fathom?' He called across to some of the other torch bearers, and they made a circuit of the pond which shone, an unbroken sheet of bluish-white ice, beneath the light of the torches.

'Is it really so deep?' Charlie asked.

'Nobody knows. My uncle fell in and was never found, and there are other stories. All rot, I expect, but traditional. Our friend Hatherley would have enjoyed them.' Roderick shivered.

'What I don't understand,' Charlie Bangs said, 'is why he didn't come with us in the morning.'

'What do you mean, old man?'

'If he wanted to go to the Post Office, he could have gone down in the carriage. He didn't want to come.'

'That's true. Can't explain it.'

They completed a circuit of the pond without seeing a break in the ice. 'Nobody's fallen in there,' Bernard said. 'It looks as though you could skate on it.'

'Perhaps there will be some news when we get back to the house.'

But there was no news. It was generally agreed that Paul must have set out for the village, got lost, and been unable to get back. Probably he had settled down at an inn for the night.

186

If nothing had been heard of him by morning, somebody would ride down to the village and make enquiries.

The affair put Sir Arthur in a bad temper. Dinner had been put back, the beef was cooked to a crisp, Bateman had forgotten to get the wine from the cellar so that it was far colder than it should have been, the whole proper routine of things had been thrown out because a pettifogging little fellow had chosen to go out for a walk in the snow. Sir Arthur muttered like a disturbed volcano throughout the meal, and went off to the drawing room with the least possible ceremony thereafter. Here Bateman, perhaps to compensate for his failure with the wine, had given orders for a good fire, and the logs were piled so high that flames shot up the chimney. Sir Arthur stood with his back to it, his head turning from side to side in a menacing manner denied by the absurdity of his little legs.

Matilda was determined not to be cheated out of her charades. 'You know how you enjoy them,' she said to her husband. 'And you are very good at them too. I won't have you being an old curmudgeon on Christmas Eve. And as a compliment to our dear son-in-law, we will play political charades. Everything must be the name of a politician, so that if you choose Sir Robert Peel, there might be one scene about a London bobby and another showing the peeling of an apple. Goodness, what's that?'

There had been a sharp crack from the fireplace. Her husband said, 'Something has happened to me.'

Gertrude rose and pointed. 'You are bleeding.'

A stain was spreading across Sir Arthur's white shirt front. He put his hand there and brought it away stained, not red but shiny blue-black. He probed inside his jacket, and came out with a sticky mess.

'It's the governor's pen. I do believe it's bust.' Roderick began to laugh, but checked himself when he saw the the looks on the faces around him.

His father was almost incoherent with fury. 'You, sir,' he said to Blader. 'This infernal instrument of yours, it's – it's typical of things today. Filthy mess all of it, a most filthy *mess*.' Because his legs were so short he scurried, rather than strode, from the room. Roderick followed him, after intercepting a look from his mother.

Blader's chubby face was dismayed. 'I don't understand. I've been using one of the pens for weeks, and had no trouble.'

'I think it must be the effect of the warmth.' Charlie took the black cylinder out of his pocket, unscrewed it, and extracted the metal tube. As he held it near the fire there was another crack, and the tube exploded, spattering Charlie's face, hands and jacket. He made an apology, and followed the others out.

'You may as well know the worst,' Bernard said coolly. 'The pen works perfectly, but if it can't be put into a warm atmosphere, it's not much use.'

He asked for a newspaper, unfolded it, removed the tube of the pen he had been given, and pushed the tube towards the fire with some care. While it was still a few feet from the blaze the tube exploded like the others, covering the paper with blue-black slime.

'You may not have invented an Everlasting Pen, but you have discovered a new firework for Guy Fawkes' Day,' Bernard said to Blader. 'Would you like to try the experiment with your own pen?'

The financier was sitting on a sofa well removed from the fire. He shook his head. 'I don't understand it. We shall have to change the formula. Just don't understand what's gone wrong.'

When Sir Arthur returned, freshly shirted, he apologised to Blader, who apologised in turn for being the inadvertent cause of so much trouble. 'Still a wonderful invention, but we shall have to change the formula a little,' he said.

'Was it the Bard who said invention breeds invention?' Matilda asked, but received no answer. 'And now we shall play my political charades.'

So they played political charades, but Sir Arthur was still simmering, and after a smooth beginning with Beaconsfield, Gladstone and Walpole, the volcano erupted, when Nelly and Charlie Bangs performed Charles Stewart Parnell, and Bernard guessed it quickly.

'Ha,' Sir Arthur said. 'Who was that? Didn't hear it properly.'

'Parnell, father, Charles Stewart Parnell, the Irish leader who's dead now.'

Her father's look was terrible. 'Dead? Of course I know he's dead. A fornicator and adulterer, a proper man to lead the Irish party.' He turned to Bernard. 'That's what you want, is it? Home Rule for the party that blows up people by dynamite, and in this country abolish the House of Lords. A club of Tory landlords is it, a gilded chamber? Let me tell you, that gilded chamber has done more for this country than any upstart coming over here and prating about freedom and prejudice ever did.'

Bernard's olive face was impassive. Dolly said, 'Father, how can you talk like that?' Matilda said that he should apologise to Bernard.

'Apologise, apologise, nothing but apologise. Other people can say what they please, but I must apologise. Very well then, I apologise, and goodnight to you all. I'm off to Bedfordshire.'

He stumped away, and that was the end of political charades. Roderick asked if anybody would like to play a hundred up before turning in, but found no takers. That was the end of an unhappy evening.

189

4 *Christmas Day: The Second Death*

Dolly's dream was disturbing. She was with Lizzie and, strangely, with red-nosed Fred. They pursued a cautious way over the waste ground beside the dye factory. 'Don't slip into the pools, they're poisoned,' Fred warned, and she saw that among the bits of rock and brick there were dark patches of water with a blue-green something shimmering on the surface. When she bent to look at the blue-green something more closely, it was revealed as a mass of large flies. Lizzie tapped her on the shoulder, and said, 'Madam, come along, madam,' Fred urged her to hurry, the shed loomed up before them. The sound of tapping grew in volume. It came from the shed, yet was associated with Lizzie's pleading voice. She was conscious of the need for action, and attempted desperately to reach the shed door, which seemed to recede as she advanced towards it.

'Madam, madam,' Lizzie cried. 'Oh please, madam.'

She sat up in bed. Beside her Bernard slept. A chink of light showed through heavy curtains. The knocking, and Lizzie's voice, continued. She put on a dressing gown, went to the door and opened it. At once Lizzie was in her arms, clinging to her.

'What's the matter, Lizzie?' Had Bateman attacked her?

'Oh, madam, he's dead and we found him, Edith and me. I don't like it here, madam, I want to go home to London.'

With her mind on Bateman, and the tale she had heard the previous day, Dolly soothed the girl, closed the bedroom door and went into the corridor. There she learned what had happened. Lizzie had been helping Edith to bring some laundry upstairs, and they had gone to use the lift, which was at the end of the main wing, where it joined the shorter section of

191

the "L". When they opened the lift door they had found a man's body. It was not that of Bateman, but, as she understood from Lizzie's semi-coherent description, the body of Paul Patterwick.

Dolly sent Lizzie to the kitchen and told her to ask cook for a cup of hot sweet tea. Then she returned to the bedroom, woke Bernard, and told him what had happened. His response was not marked by the studied calm she had come to expect of him. He got out of bed, asked who else had been told, and what had been done.

'Bernard, how should I know? Lizzie was frightened, poor girl, and came to me for comfort. What an awful thing to happen. He must have opened the door and fallen down the shaft.' He was getting dressed without washing first, something she found distasteful. 'Shall I ring for hot water?'

'No time for that now. Don't you realise that Patterwick –' He did not finish the sentence. 'Why should he have opened the door of the lift?'

'It is not far from his room, and although the doors are not the same you might mistake them. The light is poor in that corner. What else can have happened?'

He did not answer that, but went on dressing. Then he loooked up smiling. 'I'd almost forgotten. A happy Christmas to you, my dearest Dolly, our first together. Shall we exchange presents later?'

She agreed that they would do so after breakfast. When he had left her she looked at the clock on the mantelpiece, and saw that the time was nearly eight o'clock.

On the way downstairs Bernard went to look at the entrance to the lift. It was true that the light was poor, but the lift had double doors which it would have been hard to mistake for the bedroom doors, even though the handles were the same. He opened one of the lift doors and peered down, but saw only

192

blackness. The door was on a spring, so that it closed again when he let go. He could hear sounds below, and it was clear that some of the household had already been roused.

On the ground floor he found Matilda and Roderick standing beside the lift with Bateman, head drooping, in the background. The lift was of a rather primitive kind. It had a floor and three walls, and was operated by a fairly thick rope which could be pulled up and down. There was a switch which could be used as a brake, just inside the exterior double doors. Patterwick lay sprawled on the floor, his body lying sideways. Bernard knelt beside him and touched the flesh, which was cold.

'I blame myself,' Matilda said. She placed her hand on her heart. 'A bolt should have been put on the outside of this lift long ago, a good strong bolt so that it could not be operated unknowingly. Instead this poor young man opened a door and stepped out into eternity. We saw eternity the other night, as the poet says, we saw it. And all for the lack of a bolt.'

Roderick put his arm around his mother, and made consoling noises. Bernard asked whether a doctor had been sent for. Bateman moved forwards.

'I have taken that responsibility, sir. I did so as soon as I had seen for myself what had happened. I thought I should see for myself, because these young girls so often have fancies. Breakfast is served, my lady.'

Matilda said that not a crumb would pass her lips, but allowed herself to be led away by her son. Left alone, Bernard dropped to his knees and looked more closely at the body. He could see no sign of violence. He felt in the jacket pockets. They contained keys, money and an address book, which he glanced at and then returned. In the breast pocket there was a wallet, which held half-a-dozen visiting cards and some banknotes. He was about to get up when he thought of the hip pocket, and with some distaste turned the body so that he could reach it. As he did so, something rolled across the floor. In the hip pocket he found a piece of paper with writing on it. He read this, took out his own wallet and put the folded paper inside. Then he picked up the object that had rolled across the lift floor. This was one of Blader's Everlasting Pens, still intact, no doubt because it had not been exposed to heat. He put the pen in his own breast pocket, and stood up. His expression was gloomy. He went in to breakfast.

Sir Arthur's view of the tragedy was that such things were part of modern life. If you had young men sitting at desks all day, fiddling about with files, what was to be expected but that they should fall down lift shafts and so spoil Christmas for other people? He did not put it in quite that way, but he had not forgotten the annoyance and humiliation of the previous evening, and complained that the eggs were overdone.

Matilda took a third piece of toast. Bateman tottered away to supervise preparations for the Christmas meal. 'You must remember the tragedy that has been discovered this morning. It is natural that the household should be a little topsy turvy. I don't think that you should blame Bateman.'

'Said nothing about Bateman. Very loyal servant, Bateman. Don't see why the eggs should be overdone, that's all.'

'A modern hydraulic lift would have made the tragedy impossible,' Blader said. 'They make them now with a device which stops you opening the door unless the lift's actually there waiting for you.' He added that they had one installed in their own home.

'How wonderful,' Matilda said. 'Although whether the expense would be justified – it is a lift for luggage – but of course, anything that would prevent such a truly tragic event . . .' Her voice died away, then revived. 'I do hope, though, I do strongly feel that we must do our best to keep up the spirit of Christmas. I think your poor young friend would have wished it,' she said to Roderick.

Dr Riddell was a bluff old gentleman, red faced and white-whiskered. He might have resented being called out to a case in the village on Christmas morning, but a visit to Chadderley House was another matter. After he had examined the body he took a glass of sherry in the drawing room, said that the weather was seasonable, and that there was a slow thaw which was the kind he liked to see. Not so many frozen pipes, not so many running noses.

Sir Arthur nodded. 'About this poor young fellow, not going to be a great how-d'ye-do over it, I hope.'

'Dear me, no, I see no reason for that. There must be an inquest, you know, but there can be no doubt the death was an unfortunate accident. If I may venture to suggest it, perhaps a bolt should be put upon the lift doors.'

'It will be done as soon as we can get the locksmith,' Matilda said.

'What was the cause of death, doctor?' Bernard asked.

'Cause of death? Why, dropping twenty feet or thereabouts, of course. He might have got away with no more than broken bones, but the poor fellow fractured his skull. I noticed you have a braking device in the lift with a big metal switch on it. Very likely he knocked his head against that. In any case, he fractured his skull.'

'Can you give us any idea when he died?'

Dr Riddell pulled at his white whiskers. 'Bless my soul, I'm a country practitioner, not a London specialist. I can tell you he'd been dead quite a while, since rigor had set in. Certainly more than twelve hours, perhaps as many as eighteen, I couldn't be sure.'

'What did you have in mind, Bernard?' Blader asked.

'I wondered why he hadn't started out to walk to Chadderley village, since he asked Bateman how to get there, but perhaps it's of no importance.'

195

'Let the dead past bury its dead,' Matilda said. 'It was good of you to come out on Christmas morning, doctor.'

Dr Riddell said that it was a pleasure to have the family down at Christmas, added that he would make the necessary arrangements with the undertaker, and was gone.

Then it was time to go to church. A makeshift job had been done on the shaft of the brougham, the slow thaw had made the roads more easily negotiable, and the two carriages, brougham and victoria, took them to Chadderley church for matins.

In jovial mood Blader would refer to his confidential clerk Theodore Winter as his good right hand, at other times he called him an old fogey, but the clerk's devotion to all Blader enterprises and to the governor himself was not in doubt.

Winter was a thin dry little man of sixty or thereabouts, who lived alone in a couple of rooms off the Gray's Inn Road. He had never married, had worked in one or another firm of stockbrokers or bankers for the whole of his adult life, and had been with the governor now for some years. Fidelity to Blader allowed him to accept reconstruction schemes without a qualm, but he viewed all other persons or organisations with suspicion, and he had felt doubts about Duncan J. Hatherley from the beginning. Hatherley was an American, and in Winter's eyes Americans, like Frenchmen and Italians, were out to cheat the simple, straightforward British. He had been prepared to make that speculative purchase of Siberian gold shares, and Winter distrusted all those who bought speculatively. When those other companies like Lever Chain Bicycles were added to the gold shares, the confidential clerk's suspicions deepened. He had made his doubts known to Blader.

'It's not right, governor.'

'What's wrong about it? He pays on the nail, his money's good, everything goes through without any fuss or bother. I'll tell you what's wrong, Theodore my lad, you're an old fogey, and that's the only thing wrong.'

To be called by his first name was a mark of favour, something that happened no more than a few times a year, but Winter's suspicions were not allayed. He could smell something wrong, and he felt it even more strongly in the days before Christmas when he became aware that the shares in Siberian Gold Mines, Lever Chain Bicycles and some of the other stocks Hatherley had bought were coming on to the market at low prices. Somebody was selling the market short, but if it was Hatherley, what motive could he possibly have for selling at a lower figure than the one at which he had bought?

Theodore Winter did not celebrate Christmas, although there had been a time when he did. He had lived with his sister, who was unmarried like himself, and at Christmas she cooked a piece of pork and made a small plum pudding and a cake which she decorated with a figure of Father Christmas. His digestion was poor, and the unusual fare upset him for days, but while his sister was alive he kept up a pretence that he enjoyed the food. She had been dead now for a long time, and Christmas was simply another day in the year to him, although unfortunately one on which the offices were closed even though there was work to be done.

He himself went to the office, walking from his rooms as he usually did. Post was delivered on Christmas Day so that there would be letters for sorting, as well as proofs of a new prospectus for some recently-merged companies to be checked. To anybody else the rooms would have seemed cheerless, but to Theodore Winter they were more nearly home than the place in which he lived. He collected the post, took it to his cubbyhole of an office next door to the governor's, and settled down

197

happily. A few minutes later he sat staring at a communication which confirmed his worst suspicions. He muttered to himself as he read the letter again and again: 'I told him, I said to the governor he should be careful, oh dear me, I told him, an old fogey he says to me, Theodore you're an old fogey, oh dear me, and on Christmas Day too, I told him.'

He wrote the telegram with a trembling pen, the detachable cuffs he wore slipping down over his veiny old hands. Then he went out, locked the outer door carefully, and made his way to the Lombard Street Post Office, which was the nearest one to be open on Christmas Day.

Crime does not cease at Christmas, and Moss greeted several of his colleagues on the way to his room at Scotland Yard. Some of them made jokes about it being far from a merry Christmas for them, and mentioned noses kept to the grindstone, but he knew that, like himself, most of them had little objection to their lot.

His first concern was to ask whether there was news of the Irishmen, but the watch at the ports immediately ordered had so far drawn a blank. The chances were that they would have boarded a boat within an hour or two of setting their infernal machines, and be on their way across the Atlantic by now. At least he had foiled their dynamiting plans – what a sensation it would have been if they had succeeded in blowing up part of Woolwich Barracks. And, better than this, the sticks of dynamite had been traced to a firm in the East End docks area. The place had been raided, and some known revolutionaries who were friendly with workers at the place had been arrested.

That was satisfactory, but Ross's connection with the affair, and with the death of Settleby, nagged at him like an aching tooth. Suppose the man had been acting as an agent of the Irishmen, and knew where they were hiding, or the boat they had taken? Suppose Patterwick had learned something, and was waiting until the holiday was over to get the information to him? He could not expect a reply from his second cable about Ross's background for two or three days, perhaps longer. Why not go down, confront Ross with the facts, and ask for explanations he had not been given at the previous interview? Had not his maxim always been that cases are not solved by office work, writing letters, or even sending cables, but by asking questions and checking the answers? He ate a hurried lunch in one of the nearby pubs, and set out for Kent.

Blader had returned from church in low spirits. On the previous night he had tested his own pen, the one given to him by Harris, that wonderful first Everlasting Pen, by placing it near to the fire in his bedroom. The fire had been lighted early in the evening, and so had died down to gleaming embers, but the pen exploded like the others. It looked as if the pen was no use, or at best as though Harris would have to go back and start again. And he had given the man five hundred pounds! He had been disquieted also by a conversation after breakfast with Bernard Ross, when Bernard had asked him whether he had done any business with Hatherley.

'I certainly have, my boy. The man's a real speculator, knows what he wants and goes out for it. They call him Lucky Hatherley in the States. You've heard of him?'

'Yes. What kind of business did you do?'

'He bought a lot of shares, some of which I was pleased to get rid of, paid for them all on the nail. I wish I did business like that all the time. You don't mean to say there's anything dodgy about him?'

'I didn't say that.' Bernard spoke carefully, as if he were answering a ticklish Parliamentary question. 'He has the reputation of being a sharp customer, that's all.'

199

It was not a reply that could be said to be cheering. What was he doing down here, in this cold dark inhospitable house, when he could have been sitting comfortably in his drawing room at Crossways, with lighting available at the press of a switch, and the telephone ready to hand?

Bernard and Dolly exchanged presents. She exclaimed with pleasure at her diamond and ruby pendant, and waited nervously as he unwrapped her gift, an ebony writing case ornamented with mother-of-pearl. He ran delicate fingers over it, then looked up with the smile that left her unsure whether it held love or mockery.

'How well you know my taste for the discreetly flamboyant. Any letter written with this case open on my desk is bound to assume some literary style.' He kissed her, then fastened the pendant round her neck. She looked at herself in the glass on the dressing table, which of course was in the darkest part of the room. He said that it suited her perfectly.

'I never know whether you mean what you say, but it's beautiful.' She saw him behind her in the slightly flecked glass, his face abstracted. 'Bernard, you believe there is something mysterious about that young man's death, don't you? Is it to do with Mr Hatherley?'

'Hatherley? Not so far as I know.'

'But there *is* something mysterious?'

'Of course there is. Why did Patterwick want to go down to the village yesterday afternoon? Why did he not go down with the rest of you in the morning?'

'Well?' He said nothing. 'Tell me, please. You know that I hate mysteries.'

'I can't tell you. I am trying to decide what I should do. The first lesson one learns as a politician is that all action is dangerous, and that if you leave troubles alone they generally go away.'

'Then leave it alone.' she said impatiently. 'And stop trying to look like the sphinx.'

'Is that what I look like?' He took his hands from her shoulders and spoke softly. 'I doubt if I can leave this trouble alone.'

When they went downstairs they found the rest of the party in the drawing room. Blader was looking at the financial pages of *The Times*, his wife sat beside him gazing into space, Nelly and Charlie Bangs were whispering to each other just beside the conservatory, and Matilda was telling her husband and Roderick of the improvements she intended to make at Chadderley, including the installation of a bathroom in each wing, and a hot air system which would obviate the need for fires in the bedrooms. An aura of gloom pervaded the room, an air extending to the fire, which smouldered so sullenly that it might not even have made an Everlasting Pen explode.

'We shall do nothing of the kind,' Matilda's husband said, with a sharpness quite unlike his usual tone in speaking to her. 'It's all nonsense.'

'Cronin is here.' The voice was Bateman's. He stood in the doorway, head gallantly raised. 'He would like the privilege of a word, my lady. I am sorry to say that Mrs Jukes . . .' His head drooped, and the rest of the sentence was inaudible. Matilda rose, sailed majestically out of the door, and went out with Bateman.

'Cronin is the undertaker,' Dolly said in a low voice to Bernard. 'And Mrs Jukes is the cook. She drinks.'

Matilda returned with her composure slightly ruffled. 'Cronin has reminded me that of course we must inform the young man's parents. Roderick, I think you said that his father was a judge.'

'Patterwick the hangman, they used to call him. His mother's dead. Don't know their address, I'm afraid.'

Bernard suggested that his address would be found in *Who's Who*, and Roderick went off to look it up, and send a boy off with a telegram.

'And I fear that our dinner will be delayed a little. Unfortunately the cook has been taken ill.'

'Why not say she's drunk?' Dolly asked. 'I suppose it means that some things will be burnt to a cinder and others will be almost raw. But that won't be much of a change.'

'There will be a little delay,' her mother said with dignity.

Bateman tottered in, followed by a footman carrying decanters of sherry and madeira, together with a tray of biscuits which were certainly burnt. Glasses were filled, and a toast drunk to Christmas. Blader sipped his sherry, and thought longingly of Crossways, where a couple of bottles of champagne would have been open, and everybody would have been merry and bright.

Bateman appeared again, carrying an envelope on a salver. 'A telegram, my lady,' he quavered. 'For Mr Blader.' He raised his head, saw Blader's position in the room, and shuffled in that direction. Blader took the envelope, and with a muttered word of excuse tore it open.

'The boy can take back a message to Judge Patterwick,' Matilda said. 'Bateman, please make sure that he does not leave without it. Mr Roderick is writing it in the study.'

Blader put the telegram in his pocket. Bateman wavered in front of him.

'Joe, he's waiting to know if there's any answer.'

'No answer.' The financier got up and left the room. Bernard, after a moment's hesitation, followed him. Blader sat in his bedroom, staring out of the window at trees and bushes losing their whiteness with the thaw. He turned when he saw the door open.

'A sharp customer, you said. The man's a damned villain.'

'What has happened?'

'He paid for the stocks he bought with bonds supposed to have been drawn on Rothschild's. The first was genuine, the rest were forgeries. There was an acceptance date missing on one of them, the bank returned it to Rothschild's for completion, and learned it was a forgery, an excellent one, Rothschild's said. Then they checked the rest.'

'In the meantime he sold the shares he had bought from you for whatever he could get on the market?'

'Yes. Winter thought there was something wrong.'

'It's a trick he has played before. He has quite a reputation in the States.'

'The losses will be enormous. And I shall be a laughing stock in the City,' Blader said.

'Well now, governor, the losses are chiefly on paper.'

'How do you make that out?' Blader's look had something sly about it.

'You told me some of the stocks you'd sold to him, and they're mostly in fairly shaky companies, wouldn't you agree? Or to use your own words, you were pleased to get rid of them. So you've given away some parcels of shares for nothing, but it can't be called too much of a financial loss, except on paper.' Blader pouted sullenly like an overgrown child, but did not contradict him. 'If you remember that the first bond was genuine, I should say that any figure put on your actual loss would be a low one. And as for being a laughing stock, that's a matter for you. If you go to the police and the whole thing is made public, then you'll certainly look silly. But you need not do that.'

'You mean, let him get away with it scot free? I'm not doing that.' Bernard shrugged. 'You think I should?'

'You should consult your own interest. To make it public is bound to damage the share prices, or at least it won't help them.'

'The nerve of the man, coming here to tea, calling me his counsellor and friend, making a special call to say goodbye. That's what I can't get over.'

'He's renowned for having a good nerve.'

'You talk like somebody who knew him.'

Bernard said coolly, 'I told you I knew of him, and that he has a reputation in the States. I suppose things became too hot for him over there, and he decided to try his luck here. He is known as a skilled engraver, and either he brought the bonds over with him or he had access to a press over here.'

'What you say about doing nothing goes against the grain, but it might be good advice.' Blader ceased to pout, and became again something like his usual smiling self. 'I'll say this for you, Bernard, you see further through a brick wall than most. But I still want to get back to London. Do you think our hosts would take offence if we left tomorrow?'

'I feel sure they would be happy to see this Christmas party break up as soon as possible. I must leave myself in a couple of days – we are only allowed a few days of freedom and your telegram will be a sufficient explanation.'

Christmas dinner was very much what might have been expected after the collapse of Mrs Jukes. The sauces suffered particularly, the bread sauce for the turkey showing only too plainly the marks of its origin, and the Cumberland sauce for the ham and tongue tasting like liquid salt. The pudding and mince pies, however, were only slightly burnt. The crackers had been put into a damp cupboard by Bateman, and so failed to crack. A suggestion of Roderick's that they should go out and skate by torchlight on the Hundred Fathom got a mixed reception. Nelly said that it would be fun, and Charlie supported her, but Dolly called the idea ridiculous.

'You know perfectly well that there is a thaw, Roderick.

Somebody might fall in and be drowned.'

She spoke so decisively that the idea was dropped, but when the ladies had left them Roderick mentioned it again. He had drunk a good deal of wine, and was on his second large glass of port.

'Charlie, Bernard, what d'you say? There are skates out in the boot room, enough for everybody. We always skate on the Hundred Fathom when the ice is thick, used to race across it, devilish good fun. I'll race anybody for a tenner, give you a few yards start, what d'you say?'

'Suppose the ice breaks?' Bernard asked.

'Won't break. If it did we'd get a ducking, that's all.'

His father had hardly spoken since the ladies had left them. Now he said harshly, 'The pond is dangerous. You know men have drowned there, and the bodies were not recovered.'

'That's all rot, old wives' tales. Nobody drowned there for the last twenty years, don't believe all that ancient history. Old Paul wouldn't have said no, he was a sport.'

'I absolutely forbid it.'

'Oh, very well, but I don't call it much of a Christmas, sitting round doing nothing.'

A footman entered, handed Sir Arthur a card, and then bent over him. When the man had left the room Sir Arthur glowered at them all.

'There is a fellow here from the police, who says his name is –' He consulted the card. '– Moss. Apparently he has travelled down from London. He has asked to see Patterwick. I shall speak to the man and tell him his journey has been wasted.' He looked at Bernard. 'Apparently he also has business with you.'

Bernard said calmly, 'Then I had better come with you.'

The Inspector's journey had not been pleasant. There had been a long wait outside Canterbury, he had missed the connection and been forced to wait two hours for another, and it had been difficult on Christmas Day to get a cab up from Elham. Standing now in the hall of Chadderley House, he was not quite the Detective Inspector who was a powerful figure at the Yard, or the man who tracked down anarchists and dynamiters so implacably. The hall was draughty and fireless, but everything spoke of money, the old brown pictures on the walls, the heavy dark furniture, the silver tray that the footman had placed casually on the hall table. Moss had been in grand houses before, much grander ones than this, but on those occasions he had been assigned to protect an important politician, or some other figure whose life had been threatened. Now he had come to ask what might be awkward questions, and there was something a little unnerving about the prospect. Through the gloom of the hall he saw a little man bustling towards him, with the taller figure of Bernard Ross behind him. Where was Patterwick?

'You're this – Detective Inspector Moss,' Sir Arthur said, looking again at the card.

The Inspector understood that he was being addressed by the owner of the house, and acknowledged his identity.

'I suppose you know you're a confounded nuisance. I hope you've got a good reason for making this disturbance on Christmas Day.'

'A very good reason, sir, relating to the arrest of enemies of the realm. But with respect, if I may say so, I did not wish to disturb your family. It was Mr Patterwick and Mr Ross I wished to interview.'

'Can't speak to Patterwick. He's dead, poor fellow.'

'Dead?' Moss echoed incredulously.

His shocked face impressed Sir Arthur, who led the way to his study, which with a good fire going, a rack of pipes on the desk, and pictures of rowing eights and University cricket teams on the walls, was the most homely room in the house.

There Moss sat in silence after being told the details of Paul's death. Then he said, 'I take it the body has been removed.'

'Of course it has. You don't suppose we'd leave it in a goods lift?'

'No, of course not. Would it be possible for me to examine the lift, and the place from which he fell?'

'What the devil for? I won't have any detective work going on in this house, I can tell you that.'

Bernard spoke for the first time. 'Inspector Moss also wanted to speak to me. Perhaps I may be able to answer some of the questions he would have asked Patterwick. No doubt you will have understood already that the Inspector's visit is concerned with Irish affairs, and I'm sure you'll realise that it must be something important that takes him away from home on Christmas Day.'

Sir Arthur looked from one to the other of them. 'Very well, I'll leave you together. See that he has something to eat, Ross, when you've finished your talk.' He nodded to the policeman and stumped off. The Inspector found himself getting up from his chair as Sir Arthur left the room, and then silently cursed his own show of deference.

Bernard watched him with amusement. 'I gather an impression that you think there might have been something strange about Patterwick's death. I suggest you come with me and look at the lift.'

They inspected the interior on the ground floor, then went up. Moss examined the lift doors.

'Yesterday after lunch Patterwick asked the best way to walk down to the village, but he never started out. His bedroom is two doors along on the same side of the corridor as this lift. He is supposed to have opened one of these lift doors absent-mindedly, mistaking it for his bedroom – the light here is bad, as you can see – and then stepped into space, fallen and fractured his skull. There is no doubt that he died of a fractured skull, according to the local doctor.'

'I should like to look at his bedroom.'

In the room Moss looked at Patterwick's clothes and in his cases, but found nothing that had any connection with his work in the Irish section. Then he said, 'Hallo, what's this? Shine that lamp this way, if you please.'

By the light of one of the oil lamps Bernard had sent for, Moss was looking at a place near the door where the carpet ended, and gave way to parquet flooring. There appeared to be scratches on the parquet, some of them quite deep, and becoming more apparent towards the door. The detective opened the door and exclaimed in disappointment as he saw that the whole of the passage was carpeted. He looked about the room, in the wardrobe, under the bed, on the mantelpiece. Bernard followed him with the lamp.

'There? Do you see that?' With the lamp raised it was possible to see dust on the mantelpiece, and an indentation in the dust. 'A slackly run household with that much dust on the mantelpiece, but something was standing there.' He looked round. 'What do you say to this?'

On the dressing table stood a heavy brass paperweight in the form of an eagle, on a thick brass base. Moss picked it up, and stood the base on the indentation in the dust, where it fitted perfectly. He held the paperweight close to the light, then put it down with a murmur of disappointment.

'Do you know what my idea is, Mr Ross?'

'I think so. You are doubtful about the story of Patterwick opening the lift door. You believe it possible that he was killed here in this room, hit over the head with the brass eagle. You were looking at the eagle in the hope that there might be a mark on it, and were disappointed to find nothing. Your idea is that the body might have been dragged to the lift and thrown down, the marks on the parquet flooring showing where it was dragged.'

'Very clever. I take it you'd come to the same conclusion?'

'I hadn't noticed the eagle paperweight, but the idea had occurred to me. The point is, however, that without other evidence it is a possibility, nothing more. Since you didn't know of Patterwick's death, I suppose it is likely you have that other evidence, to provide a reason for his death.'

How the devil had it come about that the fellow was asking *him* questions? Moss wondered. He said curtly that there were things he wanted to know, and Ross took him back to the library.

'I saw Patterwick a day or two before he came down here. Perhaps he talked to you about that?'

'He asked me some questions. I saw no need to answer them.' Bernard took a cigarette from his case, lighted it. 'He told me that you had asked him to send a cable to the States, requesting details of my background there.'

'He did? Then I'm sure it won't surprise you to hear that I received a reply saying that no family with your name was known in the place where you were supposed to have lived as a child, nor of an uncle with your name who owned a fancy goods emporium in Chicago.' Ross did not comment. Moss's bulldog jaw stuck out. 'And perhaps it will be no surprise to be told that an attempt was made by your Irish friends to blow up Woolwich Barracks. I'm happy to say it was foiled, and I hope you're as happy to hear it.'

'Indeed I am. But I must correct you. Devas and company are no friends of mine. Do you know why I think they came to see me? Because they knew you were watching them, and wanted to persuade you that they were friendly with me. I wish you luck in catching them.'

'How do you know that they aren't already under lock and key?'

209

'Oh come now, Inspector. Would you be down here if they were?' He tapped the ash off his Abdulla, a gesture that for some reason infuriated Moss.

'I must ask you to tell me exactly where you were brought up, and what you were doing, as a young man in America.'

'And I must tell you, as I told Patterwick, that it is none of your business, with the assurance that the answer would have no connection at all with your investigation.'

'That's no answer at all.'

'But the only one you will get.'

The Inspector got up and stood with his legs straddled, his square powerful body pushed forward, a bulldog about to leap. 'I don't think you understand your position, Mr. Ross. Eustace Settleby is killed, and your address is found in his pocket. These dynamiters, revolutionaries, whatever you like to call 'em, pay you a visit, and you give me a cock and bull story about them trying to bribe you. They're getting information that enables them to clear out without being caught, even when we have advance information about their plans. Then Patterwick comes down here and talks to you, as you've admitted. Whatever he did or didn't learn from you, it's enough to make him want to send me a telegram. Before he can get down to the Post Office, however, he dies. You were clever enough to follow my ideas back there in his bedroom, but you could have had the best of reasons for knowing about that eagle paperweight.'

'Do you really believe that? Let me invite you to ponder on two points. From what you've said to me I understand that although the dynamiters got away when you hoped to trap them, they had no success at all in their dynamiting. The other point is in the form of a question. Paul Patterwick and I had our talk, such as it was, on the night before Christmas Eve, yet he didn't decide to go down to the village until the afternoon of the next day, although he could easily have gone with a party from the house in the morning. Why not?'

'I don't care for puzzles, never have. What I know is that you won't answer my questions. I shall draw my own conclusions.'

'And put on the bracelets?'

Moss ignored the slim wrists put forward, ignored the smile. 'I shall want to talk to you again, sir, just as soon as I hear from America. When do you return to London?'

'In two or three days. And now, if you've finished making these menacing noises, may I fulfil my host's injunction, and ring for a servant to give you a meal before you return?'

By ten o'clock on Christmas night the party's spirits had sunk as low as the drawing room fire, which, in spite of efforts made under Bateman's supervision, refused to draw properly. They had played charades (avoiding those controversial politicians) and proverbs, and hidden towns in which the name of a town is hidden in a sentence, and conversations in which a particular phrase has to be introduced without being detected, but even Nelly and Roderick, the most enthusiastic game players among them, were subdued.

The Bladers had gone to bed at a quarter to ten, after Blader had made his speech about the need to return on the following day. He had prepared this with some care, and was annoyed when Matilda did no more than murmur her regrets, and her husband hardly seemed to hear what had been said. Gertrude, who had made it plain that she thought all the games foolish, had embarked on a long lecture to Matilda and Dolly about the problems involved in bringing up children, and Nelly and Charlie were whispering to each other in their customary place near the conservatory. Sir Arthur had gone to his study, Bernard was reading *The Times*, and Roderick sat with feet extended, looking into the miserable fire. The Inspector had been given cold meat and a pint of beer, served to him in Bateman's sitting room, a firm social placing whch did not surprise him, and had then left in the cab he had ordered to pick him up.

Matilda listened patiently to the law as laid down by Gertrude the young mother, or at least she appeared to listen, but Dolly became increasingly irritated.

'Really, that is such nonsense,' she said to Gertrude's observation that it was bad for children to see their parents except briefly in the morning, and for half an hour before they went to bed. 'Everybody knows nowadays that a mother should spend at least two or three hours a day with her children. Modern opinion is that she should also help them with their lessons.'

Gertrude tossed her head. 'I am afraid that I am not up with the latest views, but I do speak as a mother.' She resumed her lecture, and Dolly said that she was going to bed. Nelly at once remarked that she felt tired, and was going up. Charlie Bangs stood up and yawned. Roderick was moved to expostulate.

'It's deuced boring of you all to go off like that. Surely we can have a game of something or other?'

Bernard put down the paper, and said that he was prepared for a hundred up at billiards. Charlie rejected Roderick's suggestion of a three-handed game, but approached Matilda and asked if he might show the sketches he made of her, and the rest of them came over to look. The bold lines of the three sketches showed a different Matilda from the slightly vague image she presented to the world. In the firm set of the mouth there was something of Dolly, a wildness in the eyes suggested her younger daughter, and there was strength and determination in the poised hands.

'Dashed clever, old man, but not much of a likeness,' Roderick said. 'Don't think it does you justice, mamma.'

'Flatterer,' Matilda said, but she smiled.

212

'I'm not so sure,' Dolly said consideringly. 'It's the face of somebody who gets their own way, and you know, mamma, you usually do get your own way in the end.'

'They are what Charlie sees as your true self.' Nelly put the sketches side by side. 'You've got off lightly. He makes most people look perfectly dreadful.'

Charlie said that he would be honoured if she would accept them, and Matilda replied that she would treasure them. 'The artist's portrait unlocks the door of the soul,' she said. None of them could be sure whether or not she was quoting, but the remark sent Roderick and Bernard to the billiard room, and the rest of them off to bed.

'You're pretty hot stuff,' Roderick said. 'Give me twenty-five start, and we'll have a fiver on it.'

Bernard broke, a good first shot that left both balls in baulk.

Roderick played and missed. 'You're too much for me.' He had brought the whisky decanter with him, and poured drinks for them both.

'I think perhaps I am.' Bernard sipped his drink. 'Why did you do it in the first place, Roderick? It can't have been for the money alone, that just can't have been worth it.'

'What the devil are you talking about?'

'I know the truth. I know you killed them both.' Roderick's noble head was raised arrogantly, but his eyes were frightened. 'I know the truth, but like the British with Ireland, I'm not sure what to do about it.'

When the other began to interrupt, he raised his voice. The tone had something compelling about it, the kind of quality opponents had noticed in Parliament, that made Roderick put down his cue.

'Just listen to me, and I will tell you what happened, or most of what happened. Then we can decide what should be done.'

*

Dolly was brushing her hair, something that she enjoyed doing herself, when there was a tap at the door. Her sister came in, looking both excited and unusually nervous.

'Dolly, you know you said yesterday that I should be more circumspect –'

'And you called me an old maid, or said I talked like one. I think perhaps you were right and I was wrong.'

'Dolly, do be quiet. *Or,* you said, Charlie and I should get engaged. Well, we're going to do that. Charlie will speak to father tomorrow.'

'Oh Nelly, how wonderful.' They embraced. 'He's such a nice young man. And a clever artist.'

'Of course father won't like it. Can you imagine, first a Liberal politician and then an artist. We shan't be able to marry for ages, though. Charlie says he must be able to keep me, and goodness knows when he'll be able to do that. I wanted to go and live with him, but he seemed to think that wouldn't do. I say, Dolly?'

'Yes?'

'About marriage. It is all right, isn't it? I mean, you were always independent. But you like being married, don't you?'

Dolly considered it. 'There are drawbacks but yes, on the whole it's all right. I like being married.'

'On Christmas Eve I played billiards with Patterwick,' Bernard said. 'He told me about his work for the Irish section, how proud he was of his filing system, and that he was worried because the Irish always seemed to be a step ahead of him. He thought I might be responsible, in part because he knew Devas and his friends had been to see me, and in part because he'd been told by Inspector Moss that my name had been found in Eustace Settleby's pocket. That disturbed me too, because I

214

couldn't explain it, and I always like to have an explanation for events, even though I may keep the knowledge private.

'When I went to bed I thought about what had been said, and recalled something Nelly had told me about her evening at the Anarchist Club, and the row that took place there. On the following morning I got her to repeat the story to me in rather more detail. Settleby had said that Devas was already acquainted with the Detling family. He was going on to give details when the Irishmen attacked him, and there was a fracas which ended with people being thrown out. Why had the Irishmen been so eager to stop Settleby talking? Could it be that you were the other member of the family they knew, and that you were passing them information? I remembered that you were a gambler, and that Devas was one too. If he had met you, learned your identity and something of your debts, and been told that you worked in the Home Office, might he not have approached you and offered to pay for any information you could give him? There would be no need to meet, the information could be passed to an acquaintance of his named Settleby. But this seemed a far-fetched idea, because as I said to you earlier, he surely couldn't have offered enough to make you feel it worth while. But at that point I remembered you'd shown that you knew Settleby's studio.'

'What do you mean? That's nonsense.'

'I'm afraid not. When we were talking about coming down to Chadderley, you were joking with Nelly about going to parties in studios. Disgusting studios, you said, everything piled higgledy-piggledy on tables, and not even a proper bedroom. Nelly told me that was a perfect description of Settleby's studio. When did you ever go into a studio like that?'

'It was just talking. I'm not going to listen to any more of this damned rot. If we're not going to play billiards, I'm for my bed.' He had been leaning against the billiard table. Now he turned to rack his cue.

'Roderick.' The word was spoken in the voice of a trainer bringing a dog to heel. 'I have more to say. If you go out of this room now, you will drive me to a course of action we shall both regret.'

Roderick stood uncertainly for a moment, then poured more whisky into his glass. 'All right, if you make such a beastly point of it. But I'm going to bed in half an hour, whatever you say. I'm feeling fagged.'

'I shall have finished before then. So the idea that roamed around my head ran like this. Settleby was a wonderful villain. Inspector Moss told me he was a police informer. At the same time he was in the pay of the Irish, passing on to them information he got from you about police intentions, after you had learned it from your friend Paul, either in conversation or by sneaking a look at his files. And then when he learned your background, it occurred to Settleby that he could get money from you. Blackmail you, in a word.

'He was paid very little as a police informer. No doubt the Irish were more generous, and you must have been a little goldmine. The least punishment you would face was dismissal, the greatest a prosecution for treason. So it would have been your money that provided the champagne for his party, the backing for his show. I should guess that he had my name because he learned that I was your brother-in-law, and he thought he could blackmail me as well. He was truly wonderful in his way, Eustace Settleby. But he went too far. You lost your temper and killed him.'

'Moonshine.' Roderick waved his glass, and a little whisky slopped out. The lamps shone over the green baize, but the leather sofa on which they sat was dim, so that Roderick's face was half in shadow. 'Moonshine, talk, you always were a clever talker. Nothing that can be proved. I mean, none of it's true.'

216

'I'm coming now to the question of proof.'

Dolly settled herself comfortably in bed, and waited for
Bernard to come. There would be things to tell him – and, yes,
things to ask him too, questions she was determined to have
answered. The more important matters, though, were the
things she had to tell him, the news about Nelly and Charlie,
and the news. . . she felt her eyes closing. What a bore it was
that at Chadderley there were no lamps which enabled you to
read in bed without straining your eyes.

'Proof,' Roderick echoed unbelievingly. 'Do you mean the
Inspector. . . ' He did not complete the sentence.

   'The bulldog is an admirable animal, and is said to be intelli-
gent, but I don't know that his reasoning faculties range far
beyond reaction to the sight and smell of food, and to the
sound of his master's voice. Inspector Moss is your British
bulldog. He suspects that Patterwick's death was not
accidental, but as yet has gone no further than suspicion. He
believes that Paul was attacked in his bedroom, struck on the
head there, the body dragged out to the lift when he was found
to be dead, and thrown down the well in the attempt to make it
seem an accident. He suspects, but without help is not likely to
prove. He has not seen this.' He held between finger and
thumb an Everlasting Fountain Pen. 'It was beneath the body.
I found it there.'

   'The governor gave it to him.'

   'No. There were four pens. One was given to Sir Arthur, the
others to Charlie Bangs, to you and to me. Three of them
exploded on Christmas Eve. The fourth was yours. It must
have dropped out of your pocket when you threw Paul down
the lift shaft.'

   Roderick's voice shook. 'Prove it, you just bally well prove it. What were you doing anyway, poking about at the body? That seems damned suspicious to me.'

'I did so because I thought at once that the death was not an accident.'

'I know what happened. I gave my pen to Paul, he borrowed it. And you can't prove anything else.'

'Oh yes, I can.' Bernard shook his head. 'You were using that pen for our billiards tournament, to note down the scores and the handicaps, and I shall not be the only person to remember that. If it is any consolation to you, I doubt if you really intended to kill Paul. Let me give you what I believe is known in France as a reconstruction of the crimes.

'You are an inveterate and unsuccessful gambler. When you were offered money for what must have seemed the trivial matter of passing on information from Paul Patterwick's files or from his desk, perhaps you were attracted by the risk of what you were doing as well as by the money. Perhaps you salved your conscience by reflecting that your information didn't help the dynamiters to succeed in what they were attempting, but only gave them a sporting chance of getting away. So you gave information to Settleby which he passed on verbally. He kept the papers in your handwriting, and began to blackmail you, so that the money went out as fast as it came in, or perhaps faster. Settleby was the kind of man who would want to squeeze all the juice from the orange. You told him you would pay nothing more, no doubt he sneered at you, and you killed him. Then you found the papers, and destroyed them.'

Roderick said, in a voice hardly above a whisper, 'He laughed at me.'

'I can see that must have been annoying. I became involved because Settleby had my name in his pocket. His Irish friends also approached me, and offered money if I would give them information. They may have been serious, although I suspect that they were trying merely to bemuse the bulldog. Certainly his suspicions were aroused, and he communicated them to Patterwick, who two nights ago in this room almost accused me of passing on information. Then he apologised to me on the following morning. He had realised, as somebody more quick-witted would have done earlier, that much the most likely copier of his notes and memoranda was his friend Roderick. While I was in the morning room writing letters, he sat behind me drafting a telegram to Inspector Moss. I found it in his pocket. I don't think that I should trust you with it but it reads: *Strongly suspect Roderick Detling in Home Office of passing information also re Settleby please come down urgently.* Written, as you can see, with a steel pen. Come and look at it under the light. I am sure you recognise your friend's hand.'

Under the glow of the lamp Roderick looked at the piece of paper. He said only 'Yes,' then almost stumbled back to his place on the sofa.

'I come to another point I mentioned to the Inspector. Why did Patterwick not go down to Chadderley village in the morning to send his telegram, why wait until the afternoon? It can only have been because he made up his mind to speak to you before sending it, and give you a chance to explain. He asked you to ˀome to his room. You did so, in one of the periods durinь ᴛhe tournament when people drifted in and out, and when he confronted you with the truth you killed him.'

'I never meant –' Roderick began to weep. The tears rolled down his cheeks, he looked pleadingly at his companion. 'He said such dashed unpleasant things to me, and we were friends, they upset me. Friends shouldn't say such things. But you're right, I never meant to – ' He seemed unable to say the word.

'The question that concerns me is what should be done,'

219

Bernard said in his cool voice. He waited for a comment, but none came. 'I can go to the bulldog, show him this piece of paper, tell him about the pen. There must be people who saw you when you visited Settleby, perhaps even his wife.' Roderick flinched. 'I see that you met her, and no doubt if asked she would remember you. I need hardly elaborate on the distress caused to your family by a trial for murder.' He paused, but Roderick still did not speak. 'On the other hand, you could leave the country.'

'Oh, I say, What about Gertrude, and little Billy? And I'm hard up, got no tin, you must know that.'

'I had in mind an unexpected and unexplained departure for Patagonia, with a note saying that you would send for your family later on.'

'What would I do in Patagonia?' Roderick asked piteously.

'I agree it sounds impractical, especially since you are without money. You are a great gambler, Roderick. I think you should gamble now, and lose.'

'What on earth do you mean?'

'That suggestion you made earlier about skating on the Hundred Fathom Pond. Supposing I took it up while we were playing billiards, and agreed to skate tomorrow morning. Suppose you wrote a note and pushed it under my bedroom door, saying that we'd be skating tomorrow and that you were going out to test the surface tonight. The moon is almost full, there is plenty of light.'

'The ice would bear me. I swear it's thick enough.'

'Ice was made to be broken.'

Roderick looked at him unbelievingly, then with horror. 'You devil.'

'Come now, you must see that I can't leave things as they are.'

'I don't see why not.'

'I am not prepared to rest under suspicion of murder. If you do nothing, I shall tell Moss what I know, and give him the telegram. But I hope it will not come to that. Must an outsider instruct you in the niceties of family feeling? Think of your father and mother, of your sisters. Do you want them to see you in the dock? Because it will come to that.'

'And your political career will be ruined, that's all you care about.'

Bernard stood up. 'Life is a matter of making decisions, and this one is yours. I am going to bed. I may, or of course may not, have the pleasure of seeing you in the morning.'

Bernard undressed, and when he was in his night shirt said, 'Dolly, wake up. I have something to tell you.'

'I was not asleep.'

'Your eyes were closed.'

'I was dozing, dozing and thinking. And I have something to tell *you*.'

'Very well, tell me your news first.'

She told him about Charlie's impending request for Nelly's hand, talking with unusual animation. Her looks were too determined for prettiness, but in her high-necked white night-dress with its pink lace trimmings, she looked as attractive as he had ever seen her, and he said so. She brushed aside the compliment. 'Don't you think it's wonderful? Bernard, I am so pleased. I was afraid – Nelly is such a foolish girl in some ways – but there is no need to worry now.'

'Will your father object, as he did to me?'

'I don't think so. Of course Charlie is not much of a catch, an Irish solicitor's son. But I think father has had enough of objecting. Charlie is such a nice young man.'

'Have you seen his drawings? I wonder if he is just a nice young man. I believe he is two people, like most of us. Like me.'

221

'Are you two people? I love the one I know. I have other news too.'

He was sitting on the bed, and now he took her hand. 'You say you know me, but you will know a little more tonight. Dolly, you have wondered why I was worried about the Irishmen and about Hatherley, and without telling you lies I have avoided the truth. I said that I had no past, only a future. Hatherley belongs to my past.'

'In America?'

'Yes.'

'I know what it was. When you were very young you were both members of one of those revolutionary associations, and went to prison. It is what I feared.'

He laughed. 'I have never been in prison, and hope never to do so. Cross my heart.' He took his hand from hers, and did so.

She sighed with relief. 'What then?'

'I wanted to keep this a secret from you, but I was wrong.' He paused and went on. 'Hatherley is a professional crook, a skilled forger. He specialises in fraudulent bonds, and in cheating banks and business men. When you saw him in Whitechapel he was making arrangements for the use of a small press to which, I found out by making enquiries, the man Harrison had access. Harrison himself has been in prison for making counterfeit money, and he helped Hatherley with the printing of his fake bonds. Once they were ready Harrison made himself scarce.'

'But what has all this to do with you.'

'His name is not Hatherley, it is Abe Rosenheim. He is my brother.' She said nothing. 'My family were German Jews, and they were not farmers, although it is true that they died when I was a child. The uncle who brought me up in Chicago was named Ike Rosenheim, and he was a pawnbroker.'

Still she said nothing. She could hardly take in the meaning

222

of what he said. She had never to her knowledge met a Jew socially. Her work in the East End had brought her into contact with some Jewish families, and she had noticed that they seemed to make more trouble than other immigrants, often complaining about things that aliens of other nationalities took for granted. Nationalities, she knew, was the wrong word, because a Jew could be English, French or Russian – or German. An English Jew, Mr Disraeli, had become Prime Minister, but she knew that to have been exceptional. She did not know what to say to her husband.

'He is your elder brother?'

'Yes. I knew he called himself Hatherley, and heard of him occasionally. Obviously he also knew of me, and recognised my name when he heard Blader mention it.'

'When I saw you together something worried me, I knew that there was something I should understand. Of course, it was the resemblance between you. He came to Chadderley specially to see you? He must feel affection for you.'

'In a way I think he does. But Abe is daring, reckless, not a calculator of chances like me. We haven't met since I came here years ago, and I think he genuinely wanted to see what I looked like. At the same time he enjoyed trying to frighten me with the thought that he might greet me as brother Bernie. I did not think he would do that, but I couldn't be sure. He knew that, and it amused him.'

'So he is Abe Rosenheim, and your name –'

'Is Bernard Ross. I changed it legally, by deed poll, a few months after I came here, when I realised that the answer to Shakespeare's question "What's in a name?" is "Often a great deal." Do you suppose that Bernie Rosenheim could have become a Member of Parliament?'

'You were wrong not to tell me. I have no vulgar prejudices. Many of the Prince of Wales's friends are Jewish.'

'I have heard him abused fifty times for that reason. And although my parents were of the faith, I am not a practising Jew.'

'So when I thought you were aghast at Charlie Bangs's photograph, it was your brother's visiting card that worried you?'

'Yes. I knew that he used the name Hatherley.'

'You should have told me before we were married. It would have made no difference. But you should have let me make up my own mind.'

'You are perfectly right. It has been a burden to me ever since. I feared the Irishmen knew of it and would try to use it against me, but can you imagine what your father would have said if he had known of my origins?'

She could, very easily. She had often heard her father on the subject of Jews, whom he identified solely with moneylenders. 'It would have made things difficult.'

'They were difficult enough. It would have made our marriage impossible. Do you regret that?'

'No,' she said, and knew that she meant it. 'Bernard, get into bed.' When he had done so, she said, 'You said that you calculate chances. I believe that you calculated just when to tell me this, and I have a feeling that you have still not told me all the truth. Is there nothing else?'

'Nothing about the past. You know my secret now.'

'It shall remain a secret. And that is all?'

'That is all.'

'I shall never be sure of you, shall I? But I daresay that's all for the best. Now I will tell you *my* secret.' She whispered it to him, and he expressed his delight.

Afterwards she slept peacefully, but he stayed awake for a long time, wondering whether he should have told Dolly about her brother. Politics is the art of the possible, the great Bismarck had said, and this was a precept he tried to observe, in politics and in life.

It had been time to tell Dolly about his background, for her curiosity would have discovered it in the end, as no doubt it would be discovered by the British bulldog, to whose investigations it would be irrelevant. Thinking of Moss, he wondered whether he should have told the Inspector what he had learned, rather than confronting Roderick. There would have been scandal, and scandal of a kind a promising politician could not afford. If to think in those terms was calculating, such calculations must be part of any politician's life. They do not, he thought drowsily, conflict with the desire to see justice done, for there is more than one way of doing justice. On the other hand he could not be sure of Roderick's reaction. Perhaps the strategy had failed, perhaps, perhaps. . . Then, as he was drifting down the long arcade towards sleep, he heard the sound that he had been subconsciously awaiting, the sound of something being pushed under the door. He got out of bed, saw the slip of white paper on the carpet, took it to the window, drew aside the curtain, read what was said in the moonlight, and knew that the strategy had succeeded.

So that was that. He dropped the paper where he had picked it up, and got back into bed. Dolly did not stir. Tomorrow there would be alarms, tears and reproaches when the body was taken from the Hundred Fathom Pond, but Settleby's death would remain unsolved, and Paul Patterwick's would stay an accident. The Detling secret would be preserved for ever, preserved by an outsider. Justice and self-interest are often identical, he thought, and mentally noted the phrase as one to be used at some time in a speech. With that, he fell asleep.